The door slammed.

I was alone with Kent.

He arched an eyebrow, narrowed evil eyes. I forced myself not to be scared to death.

"How long had you two been together, you and Daisy?"

"Six months."

I thought about the six months. Daisy had still been with Kit for most of that time. "Did you love her?"

Not so much as a blink from him. "Yes."

"Do you know who killed her?"

"No."

Liar. Liar. But he'd pass a lie detector test easy. "Do you think her death could be tied to the drugs she sold?"

His chair creaked as he rose. "It's time for you to leave, Nina," he said in a soft, scary whisper. "I suggest you stay out of this. Daisy was killed, and the same could easily happen to you!"

The threat was clear.

I would have run, but my knees were shaking too hard.

Nina Quinn Mysteries by
Heather Webber

WEEDING OUT TROUBLE

Heather Webber

AVON

An Imprint of HarperCollinsPublishers

This is a work of fiction. Names, characters, places, and incidents are drawn from the author's imagination or are used fictitiously and are not to be construed as real. Any resemblance to actual events, locales, organizations, or persons, living or dead, is entirely coincidental.

AVON BOOKS
An Imprint of HarperCollins*Publishers*
10 East 53rd Street
New York, New York 10022-5299

Copyright © 2008 by Heather Webber
ISBN 978-0-06-112972-8
www.avonmystery.com

First Avon Books paperback printing: August 2008

Avon Trademark Reg. U.S. Pat. Off. and in Other Countries, Marca Registrada, Hecho en U.S.A.
HarperCollins® is a registered trademark of HarperCollins Publishers.

Printed in the U.S.A.

10 9 8 7 6 5 4 3 2 1

*To everyone who looks at dirt and
sees the possibilities.*

WEEDING OUT TROUBLE

One

Thou, Nina Colette Ceceri Quinn, shall never again break and enter.

A commendable commandment if there ever was one. Don't get me wrong. I wasn't above bending the law every now and again, sneaking into somewhere I didn't belong, but I'd never actually *broken* anything to gain entrance.

Until now.

Shifting my weight, I swung a grub hoe over my head, hitting the window above my head full force.

I ducked as glass shattered.

My breath plumed in front of my face in an icy cloud.

A cold front swooping down from Canada had blanketed the Ohio Valley the night before. Forecasters predicted heavy snow to fall throughout the weekend, all but guaranteeing a white Thanksgiving in six days' time. A rarity around these parts.

Ordinarily, snow would throw my schedule into a tizzy. As a landscape designer I was at Mother Nature's fickle mercy.

Thankfully, come tomorrow, I had nothing planned, workwise, for an entire week. Plenty of time for the snow to melt and fifty degree temps to return to this area of Ohio.

But right now I had bigger things to worry about than snow.

Frost crunched beneath my Timberlands as I set the grub hoe aside, my feet leaving icy footprints amidst the almost naked shrubbery.

The building I was breaking and entering into sat far from the road, surrounded on three sides by dense woods. Absolutely no one was around. I didn't have to worry about being seen or heard by nosy passersby.

My fingers flexed inside a pair of leather gloves as I knocked away jagged glass along the window frame, clearing an opening for me to climb through.

Only one problem. How did I get in?

I attempted to lift myself, but I barely made it a foot off the ground. It might be time to give pull-ups another chance at the gym, despite the fact that I almost suffocated myself trying them before.

Stepping back, I gauged the distance to the window and took off running.

I jumped, I leapt, I fell on my ass. Hopefully the shrub I landed on had already reached dormancy and would recover.

Before I seriously hurt myself, I looked around for something to help me up and in. I wasn't exactly known for my grace. Or my height. I'm on the shorter side of five-foot-five, and the window was a good five feet off the ground.

In the end I leaned the grub hoe against the stucco exterior of the building and used the top of the hoe's handle as a foothold.

My nerves were doing a jig in my stomach as I heaved myself up and perched on the window frame, balancing precariously. The muscles in my arms burned from the strain.

Definitely time to talk to Duke, my no-nonsense personal trainer, about strengthening my upper arms.

Wind howled as I peered inside a back room of an adorable ranch-style home that had been converted into Daisy Bedinghaus's holistic therapy business, the Heavenly Hope Holistic Healing Center.

Maybe twelve-by-twelve, the interior space looked like it had once been a bedroom, converted now into a treatment room. Angled diagonally, a padded massage table took up most of the area.

Swinging my feet through the opening, glass crunched loudly as I found my footing.

I'd have to work on my B&E skills.

No, no I wouldn't.

This was the last time I was breaking and entering. It was a commandment now and forever. And once a commandment was etched onto my mental tablet, I rarely broke it.

Nothing seemed out of place. A tray of aromatherapy bottles sat on a small granite-topped counter. According to the labels, every scent from lavender to jasmine to strawberry kiwi and eucalyptus were in the small brown glass bottles neatly aligned against the tiled back splash. Stacks of pristine white towels in every size lay folded neatly on shelves above the countertop.

The door to the room was ajar, and I crept over to it, peeking through the crack.

Every few steps I'd stop and listen, but heard nothing but my own breathing.

Quickly, I checked the reception area out front, then backtracked down the hallway, sticking my head into two other treatment rooms. Both were empty.

I nearly jumped clear out of my skin as the phone on my hip rang. My current ring tone, the theme song from the *Match Game,* echoed through the empty building.

My B&E skills definitely needed honing. I'd forgotten to silence my phone. How amateurish was that?

But wait, I reminded myself. There would be no more breaking and entering, so no honing of any kind was needed.

Well, except for the muscles in my arms . . .

The phone rang a second time before I could pull it off my hip. Quickly, I checked the caller ID screen and recognized my office number. "Did he show?" I asked, hearing the panic in my voice.

That morning, Taken by Surprise, Garden Designs, my landscaping company, had started a full backyard make-over in a swanky development near the office. Kit Pipe, my full-time landscape contractor, good friend, and current roommate, had never arrived at the job site.

It was the first time in four years he'd been a no-show.

"No one's seen or heard from him," Tam Oliver said. I could hear the panic in her voice too.

The jig in my stomach commenced to a full-blown hokey-pokey, shaking all about. It hurt.

"I take it he's not there?" she asked. Tam was my part-time office manager, full-time friend, and all around go-to girl. I couldn't run my business without her. Our friend-ship was just icing. She bore an uncanny resemblance to a young Queen Elizabeth, right down to the mannerisms and elocution. Except for her down-home Kentucky accent, she'd be a dead ringer.

A hanging water feature burbled on the wall next to me; meant to soothe, I imagined.

Soothing would be nice. But only one thing would calm me now.

Finding Kit. Making sure he was okay. Something was terribly wrong. I could tell.

I leaned against the wall. "Doesn't seem like anyone is here," I told her.

For a second the ramifications of breaking and entering flitted through my head. How was I going to double-talk my way out of this? Worry for a friend just didn't seem like a good excuse.

I could practically hear Tam's nervous twitch through the phone. "And he didn't come home last night either?"

"No." I edged away from the wall. "Last I knew, he was dropping Ana off at the airport. I haven't seen him since."

"Have you talked to Ana?"

My cousin, Ana Bertoli, had a close relationship with most of my employees. At one time or another she'd been their probation officer. The people she particularly liked, she sent to me for jobs. Through the years, close friendships had formed.

"I spoke to her last night after she landed." She'd gone to California to spend Thanksgiving weekend with her mother, my aunt Rosetta, lovingly known by me as Aunt Rosa. "Nothing seemed out of the ordinary."

"I wonder why he'd gone to see Daisy?" Tam asked.

The question had gone through my head a time or two since I found Kit's Hummer in Heavenly Hope's parking lot.

Until recently, Kit and Daisy Bedinghaus had been dating for years. They'd been broken up for about a month now, and Kit and his enormous dog, BeBe, were staying with my stepson Riley and me. It was supposed to have been a temporary thing, but Kit ended up staying while trying to get his life together.

"No sign of Daisy either?" Tam asked.

"No one is here." I'd never actually met Daisy. I'd seen the back of her head once, and heard her voice because I'd been shamelessly eavesdropping, but never had a face-to-face meeting.

Kit was extremely private, and liked to keep his personal life to himself. I respected that, though my nosy side would have liked to meet the woman who broke his heart. To see if she really was as crazy as I thought. She had to be. Kit was as good a man as they came.

Tam said, "Maybe they got back together and eloped, Nina."

"Maybe," I lied. It was a nice thought, but I didn't think that was the case at all.

If nothing else, Kit was responsible. No way would he go off without telling me.

And leave his beloved Hummer behind.

Out Heavenly Hope's front windows I could see Kit's look-at-me yellow Hummer in the parking lot, covered in a fine layer of frost—it had obviously been there overnight.

I might not have broken into Heavenly Hope if not for seeing that truck there.

And spotting tiny bloodstains on the driver's seat and steering wheel.

Kit kept his car immaculately clean, so the blood had to be new. The rational part of my brain kept thinking the stains could have come from a nosebleed. Or a paper cut. And that I shouldn't overreact and call the police immediately, which had been my first instinct.

My second instinct had been to break into Heavenly Hope.

I was seriously beginning to doubt my judgment.

However, I did have some insight into police investigations. I had once been married to a policeman, and knew the police could do little at this point. Kit hadn't been missing all that long, and the bloodstains were so small they'd probably be dismissed without anything further to go on.

So I'd kinda-sorta taken it upon myself to make sure Kit wasn't inside Heavenly Hope, bleeding to death.

I must have been on speaker phone, because Ursula "Brickhouse" Krauss, my other part-time office manager, piped in. "Ach. Is Daisy's Lexus there?"

Once upon a time Brickhouse had been my high school English teacher. These days she was my full-time nemesis, all-around pain in my butt, and somewhat neighbor. In her sixties, she had short spiky white hair, ice blue eyes, and never hesitated to speak her mind. She currently had an on-off relationship with my next door neighbor, Mr. Cabrera, who loved every inch of her short, squat, brick-shaped self. Right now they were on, and I'd been seeing a lot of Brickhouse in the Mill, the nickname of the small neighborhood of Freedom, Ohio, where I lived.

There were days we actually didn't want to kill each other, but they were few and far between. One thing we did agree on was Kit.

We both adored him.

"Besides my car, Kit's Hummer is the only car in the lot."

Brickhouse clucked, a habit of hers.

And for the first time since I've known her, I felt the compulsion to cluck along with her.

Not a good sign.

"Did you try calling Daisy's house again?" I asked. No one had been there earlier when I stopped by.

"Every three minutes. He's not answering his cell either."

"It's in his truck." I'd seen it in the cup holder.

"That's not good," Tam said.

I agreed.

Tam rushed on. "I checked in with Deanna—she has everything under control at the site. Everyone's on edge, focused on getting the job done."

Deanna Parks, a novice designer, worked for me full-time. I completely trusted her to finish the job today.

"Thanks for checking with her." As the owner of TBS, a company that provided surprise garden makeovers, my clients paid me a lot of money to make sure their yards were done to perfection. Even when beloved employees went missing.

I winced as I threw open a closet door. Thank God nothing fell out.

Like Kit's body.

Quickly, I checked a small half bath and kept moving down the hallway.

"Do you think we should call the police?" Tam asked.

I knew she must have been extremely worried about Kit if she was talking about bringing in the police. Tam had an extreme dislike of law enforcement, with the one exception of her live-in love, Ian Phillips, who happened to be a DEA agent.

"I'm not sure," I said.

I heard a cluck just before Brickhouse said, "You should call Kevin."

Kevin being Kevin Quinn, my ex-husband. He was a homicide detective with the Freedom Police Department, and had recently been freelancing for Ian Phillips.

He'd been on an undercover assignment for the DEA when he was shot. Now, a month later, he was still in the hospital, recovering after a blood infection had kept him there longer than anyone expected. He'd have a few scars and would need some physical therapy but would be just fine.

Kevin was itching to get out of the hospital, eager to go home. He wasn't one who liked to sit still for any length of time, and I secretly wondered if the hospital stay was doing more harm than good.

"I'll call." My agreement to call Kevin told me just how worried about Kit *I* was.

These days I tried to steer clear of Kevin as much as possible. Being near him—especially when he was hurt and my mother hen syndrome had kicked in—tended to confuse me and stir up feelings that were supposed to be long gone, taped up, and shipped off to some small iceberg in the Bering Sea.

Mostly because I'd fallen in love with another man.

I paused outside a closed door at the end of the hall. My stomach knotted. I reached for the knob, slowly turned it. "Whoa."

"Whoa what? What whoa?" Tam's voice rose.

The room was clearly Daisy's office. My superior Clue-playing abilities had nothing to do with the revelation—the plaque on the desk in the center of the room told me so.

"Daisy's office," I said. "It's been completely ransacked. There are files and papers scattered everywhere." I spotted a computer monitor, but no hard drive. "Someone took her computer too."

"Kit wouldn't do something like that," Tam said.

"Ach. He's a peace-loving kind of guy," Brickhouse said. "It's the work of some no-good burglar. Probably one of my former students. That Marvin Partridge was never any good."

I remembered Marvin. He was a doctor now, a pediatrician. I wondered what he had done to tick off Brickhouse.

A noise came from the closet, and the fine hairs on the back of my neck stood on end. Adrenaline surged—my fingers tingled, my heart raced.

"Is anyone there?" I said softly, barely above a whisper. Suddenly I felt the need to climb underneath the desk. I refrained, telling myself I was braver than that. Or stupid, which was more likely.

"Is someone there?" Tam screeched. "Should I call the police?"

It was hard to talk. "I don't know. I hear something. Kit?"

The closet door was cracked open. Was he in there? Hurt?

The noise stopped again.

Maybe it was just the wind.

Probably.

Definitely.

I was being delusional, which broke one of my top ten commandments.

"Nina? Are you okay?" Tam asked.

"Shh," I said, then called out, "Hello? Kit?"

Bolstering my courage, I glanced into the small walk-in closet. Maybe six-by-six, the shelves and floor were covered with vitamins, herbs, and powders that had been scattered in a hasty search.

There was no Kit.

"Nina!" Tam cried.

"I'm okay," I said. "There's a closet here filled with pills and powders, looks like vitamins and supplements."

"Ach. Maybe someone thought Daisy had more hardcore stuff in there. That Marvin was a pothead, as I recall."

She was right—he had been.

And I couldn't help but think that if it had been Dr. Marvin, he'd picked the right place to burgle. Because I knew something Tam and Brickhouse didn't. Daisy was a big believer in the power of medicinal marijuana—and supplied it in and around Freedom to those in need, including the residents of a retirement home I'd done a mini for not long ago, which was how I learned of her little side business.

I couldn't help but wonder who else might know.

"They're probably in Gatlinburg at one of those cute little chapels," Tam said brightly. Her diction had slipped and a drawl had crept in. Nerves, full force.

"Ach. Probably getting their marriage license right now. Just waiting for the right time to call."

"Oh, oh," Tam added excitedly, obviously buying into the fantasy, "BeBe's probably going to wear the rings they picked out around her neck on a ribbon."

Brickhouse clucked. "Lord help the place that lets BeBe through the doors."

Tam laughed.

Kit's enormous English mastiff, easily over a hundred pounds, was an adorable, clumsy, drooling, slurping machine. The image of her in a small chapel would have been quite humorous—if I were in the laughing mood.

I wasn't.

The noise started up again, and I made a quick decision. "Go ahead and call the police, Tam," I said nervously.

"Why? Did you find something?"

No, but I was seriously creeped out. "Nothing, really. I think I'm going to wait outside."

Bravery had never been one of my strong traits, and I wasn't stupid. I was getting the heck out.

Then I heard something that ripped open my heart.

Whining.

Doggy whining.

"I'll call you two back, okay?"

"Why? Did you find something?" Tam asked.

"I'll call," I said, and flipped my phone closed.

"BeBe?" I shouted.

The scratching intensified.

Checking the closet more closely, it didn't take long to notice a crack in the wall to my right running from floor to ceiling.

I pushed and pulled. There had to be a way in there.

BeBe whined and cried, but never barked.

It took a good couple of minutes before I discovered that the rug in the corner of the closet had been lifted a bit. Beneath it, I found a small button. I pushed it and a door slid open, disappearing into the framing between the closet and the darkened room beyond.

BeBe barreled out, knocking me over. Her tail thrashed and her crying brought tears to my eyes.

It took a second for me to find my feet, another to realize someone had taped BeBe's snout shut with masking tape. I carefully took it off. Her barks split the air, and my first thought was to get her water. I took her to the bathroom I'd seen in the hallway and turned on the faucet. She drank and drank.

When she had her fill, I went back to Daisy's office.

Relief flooded me as I heard sirens in the distance. At this point, breaking and entering appeared to be the least of my problems.

Swallowing over a lump of fear, I went back into the closet, BeBe on my heels.

I had to know. Had to find out if Kit was in there too.

The darkness was overwhelming. My hand shook as I felt along the wall for a switch and finally found one. I blinked against the blinding light.

Once my vision cleared, I saw it. In the middle of the room a crumpled body laid deathly still, surrounded by small white pills.

All common sense about not touching a crime scene failed me as I knelt down. BeBe sat next to me, pawing the air, crying. I swallowed over a coconut-sized lump in my throat and checked for a pulse.

I'd finally come face to face with Daisy Bedinghaus.

Unfortunately, she was dead.

Two

Usually I was quite averse to doggy slobber, but I couldn't find the heart to push BeBe away as she continued to lick my face.

I slowed to a stop at a red light, and BeBe took one last slurp and finally settled down into the passenger seat, her giant paws dangling over the edge of the seat.

I turned up the volume on the radio a bit. Recently I'd been listening to country music, but in this time of crisis I reverted back to familiar habits. Spinning the dial, I stopped on the oldies station.

"You've Lost that Loving Feeling" was playing, but it wasn't the Righteous Brothers singing it. It was Hall and Oates.

On the oldies station.

Oldies.

Hall and Oates.

Something was very wrong in this world.

Disgusted, I flipped off the radio.

BeBe lifted her head to check and see if she was missing anything of importance, halfheartedly licked my hand, and put her head back down on her paws.

She'd had a rough day.

We'd both had a rough day.

The light turned, and I headed for home. It was one of those gray, cloudy, stay-in-bed days.

I know I wished I'd stayed in bed.

Sleet spit at the window. My wipers slashed it away. With more than a few accidents on the roadways, Freedom's police station had seemed like a ghost town. Except for the detectives covering Daisy's case.

And me.

I'd been at the station most of the day, answering the same questions repeatedly. I'd actually found myself wishing Kevin was there to run interference. I'd even found myself wishing for Ginger Barlow, aka Ginger Ho. She was also a detective. And also Kevin's live-in lover.

Reveals how desperate I was, doesn't it?

Unfortunately, Kevin was still laid up in the hospital, and Detective Darren Zalewski, fondly known in my family as "Lewy," informed me Ginger was on vacation leave. She was probably with Kevin at the hospital, playing doctor.

That thought didn't so much as twitch a nerve, which meant either I was getting used to their relationship or I had gone numb thanks to the events of the day.

I leaned toward numb. I didn't think I could ever get used to seeing Kevin and Ginger together, all lovey-dovey.

Some things just weren't possible.

But I did wish one or the other had been with me today as the detectives interrogated me for six hours without so much as a potty break for BeBe, whom I refused to leave outside.

Right now I wasn't too fond of Lewy, though I'd always liked him up until today, despite the fact that he'd been Ginger's partner before she paired with Kevin. Joe Nickerson was a good fifteen years older than Lewy, and had a reputation for being touchy-feely. Never with me, but I'd heard stories.

Freedom was a small suburb. Its police department was like a family. Lewy and Joe had been to my house many times, and Kevin, Riley, and I to theirs. However, they hadn't taken too kindly to finding me at the scene of a homicide.

What did I expect? I'd divorced Kevin—my branch had fallen off Freedom PD's family tree. They weren't cutting me any slack.

Too bad Ana had left town. I wanted to be catty, but it was no fun being catty alone.

Right now I wished I hadn't turned down her offer to go with her to Aunt Rosa's for Thanksgiving. I would have been basking in the California sun this morning instead of finding Daisy dead, presumably from that gunshot wound to her chest.

Where was Kit?

It was the question Lewy and Joe had kept asking, over and over. The one I'd kept asking myself.

I didn't know the answer. And even if I did, I wasn't sure I'd tell them.

Reaching over, I rubbed BeBe's dark ears. Exhausted, she didn't even flinch.

My mind kept going back to the secret room where I'd found Daisy. It had been lined with grow lights—obviously she was cultivating her own marijuana. There hadn't been any plants, though. Also, two industrial shelving units had been cleared out, which made me wonder what had been stored on them.

Before the police arrived, I'd managed a good look at the white pills on the floor. I even picked one up—I could always plead ignorance if the police were able to retrieve any prints from it.

One side was unmarked. The other side had an elaborate imprinted design, but it wasn't anything I could identify. It was the image of a narrow oblong shape with what looked like tunnels trailing off it.

Unusual to say the least.

I'd placed it exactly where I found it, next to Daisy's body, and hoped Lewy and Joe wouldn't find out I'd touched it. I had no doubt I'd be locked up for tampering. They weren't in the best of moods today.

I thought about what I knew so far. Daisy was dead. Kit

had been at the crime scene, and knowing him, he didn't leave BeBe there willingly.

If Kit didn't kill Daisy—and I refused to believe otherwise—then someone else knew about that room. And what had been stored in there.

Who?

In my rearview mirror I caught sight of a dark sedan following me. I could just make out that the pair of men in the front seat wore tan trench coats, collars raised to their ears.

No doubt it was Lewy and Joe. And also no doubt they wanted me to know they were watching.

Well, let them.

That's me, Nina Colette Cooperating Witness Ceceri Quinn.

In the console cup holder my silenced cell phone vibrated. I'd been ignoring calls left and right all day. My coping mechanisms had been maxed out, and I couldn't deal with the prying questions from friends and family on top of everything else.

I checked the screen, and flipped the phone open. "Hi, there."

I heard a deep inhale, a lengthy exhale. "I was worried."

"I'm all right."

"You're lying."

Turning left, I said, "Maybe."

I could hear the smile in Bobby's voice. "There's no maybe about it, Nina. Where are you?"

"On my way home. You?"

"Headed that way."

The sleet had picked up. I bumped up the speed on my wipers, turned up the heat in the truck. "How'd the interview go?" He'd been looking for a job since resigning as an elementary school principal nearly a month ago.

Static crackled. "It went."

"I'm sorry."

"Don't be. I'll find something."

Bobby MacKenna and I had been dating off and on for almost six months. We'd gotten serious fast, slowed things down, split up, and since he returned to Ohio from Florida a month ago, had been putting the pieces back together.

It took some doing, though. Especially after I found him holding another woman in his arms.

I was quite proud of myself for not overreacting to the scene, because after Kevin cheated on me, I had serious trust issues.

No one was happier than I when Bobby explained that the woman had simply been giving him a thank-you hug for returning a bracelet he retrieved from his charming geriatric klepto grandfather Mac.

Considering Mac had snitched my watch, the story rang true.

Personally, I thought the woman would have liked more of a relationship with Bobby. But he was only interested in me.

It did my heart good.

He'd moved in across the street, and we were now closer than ever.

It felt good.

And scary.

And hopeful.

I liked the hopeful part.

"How about some hot soup and a long bath tonight?" he asked.

"In that order?"

"Not necessarily."

"Care to join me?" I asked.

"You know how much I love soup."

I laughed, then instantly teared up. "Somehow it feels wrong to laugh."

BeBe lifted her head, yawned, and put it back down. The sleet was slowly turning to snow.

"I knew you weren't okay," he said.

"I'm just . . . I'm just . . . "

"Scared?"

"Terrified. They have a manhunt out for him, Bobby. Like he's some dangerous animal."

"We know he isn't."

I exhaled. I'd been holding my breath without realizing it, waiting, worried. Bobby's opinion meant a lot to me, and I didn't know what I would have done if he believed Kit guilty of Daisy's murder.

"We know," I said, "but our opinions don't count."

Bobby's voice deepened. "The police will find evidence to clear him."

"What if . . . " I took a deep breath.

"What?"

I couldn't bring myself to say it. I could barely think it. *What if he's dead?*

What if whoever killed Daisy killed him too? I shuddered. "Nothing."

"Listen, do you need a lawyer? I could call Josh."

"No!" Bobby's sleazy cousin, Josh Drake, was the last person I'd ever want representing me. "I'm good. They pretty much think Kit did it. I'm just a witness."

Bobby laughed. He knew how I felt about Josh, and I had the feeling he'd only brought up his name to get my mind off Kit for a minute. "Okay, no Josh. I've been thinking . . . "

"Uh-oh."

"No, no. It's just that with all this going on, maybe we should cancel next week."

"You, Robert Patrick MacKenna, are not getting out of Thanksgiving dinner. So stop trying."

"Have I warned you about my family?"

"I've met your grandfather and Josh, how much worse can it get?" After a second of silence, I said, "Bobby?"

"Worse," he mumbled.

I didn't believe him. His grandfather was a piece of work. And Josh was pretty darn bad.

"Thanksgiving is still on," I said. "I'll see you tonight, okay?"

"I'll bring the bubbles."

Hanging up, I glanced in the rearview mirror. Lewy and Joe still followed.

My phone vibrated again. I thought about turning it off, but looked at the ID and couldn't help myself.

"No way. Absolutely no freakin' way. No way on God's somewhat green—I hear global warming is wreaking havoc and now El Niño is back—earth. Holy hell. Not Kit. Not that big cuddly, wuddly teddy bear. Are the police idiots? They probably can't find their nightsticks with both hands, can they? Overbearing heterosexual alpha males, probably trying to assert their manliness. Am I right? Am I right?"

Perry Owens didn't wait for my answer.

"Kit's a target, that's what he is. A big six-foot-five target. Just paint big red round circles on his chest—though, ugh, he really shouldn't wear red, not his color at all—and have a little shooting practice."

I broke in before he hyperventilated. "Breathe, Perry. Breathe."

"Sorry, sugar, but I'm pissed."

I smiled. "I can tell."

"You won't tell Kit I called him a cuddly, wuddly teddy bear, will you?"

I really didn't want Perry to get his ass kicked. "Your secret is safe."

I'd met Perry Owens while Bobby and I were undercover contestants on a sleazy reality TV show. Perry and his life partner, Mario Gibbens, had been the other set of contestants. The show ended up being a nightmare, where the only realities were adultery, deceit, and murder.

The upside was that Perry, a hairdresser, and I had bonded. He'd given me a complete head-to-toe makeover, some of which I'd kept up, most of which I let go by the wayside.

"What are we going to do about it?" Perry asked.

"About it?"

"We've got to clear his name. He's probably hiding out until someone does."

"You really think he's hiding out?"

Perry must have heard what I was really asking. "Oh, sugar, don't be thinking such things. Kit's a tough cookie. No way is he kicking the bucket, feeding the earthworms—"

"You have such a way with words, Perry."

He laughed. He had a great laugh, full of sound. Infectious. "Sugar, I'd been thinking 'pushing up daisies,' but decided that might be in bad taste."

I groaned. "You're awful."

"That Daisy was no good for him, anyway. I'm sad she went the way she did, but I'm not sad she's out of his life for good."

Turning right, I inched along Tylersville Road. There were several vehicles on the shoulder of the road, abandoned. In southern Ohio, this weather always turned roadways into a dangerous game of bumper cars.

I thought about what Perry had said. About Daisy. Honestly? I agreed with him. I'd seen what she put Kit through over the last few months. But I'd also seen how much Kit cared for her. For him, I mourned her death.

But only for him.

BeBe snuffled.

And maybe BeBe too.

I loved them both.

"How about dinner tonight?" he asked.

"Can't. I have plans."

"What's that I hear in your voice?"

"Bubbles," I said.

He laughed. "I think I want details, but have to run. Mario's on the other line. I'll talk to you later. Hang in there, sugar. Everything will be okay."

I slowly turned right into the Mill. The back of my truck fishtailed a bit, but I managed to keep control.

Down the block, I could see a line of cars parked in front of my house.

I wasn't the least bit surprised. The neighborhood wasn't known as the Gossip Mill for nothing. All my neighbors would want a run-down of today's events, especially since they had gotten to know Kit over the past few weeks.

My mom, my dad, probably my sister, would want every last detail too. If my brother Peter lived within a hundred mile radius, I'm sure he'd have been waiting for me on the front porch, lousy weather and all.

We were a nosy lot, us Ceceris.

I checked my watch. I'd tell them what I knew, but come six o'clock, they were gone. Vamoosed. I had a date with bubbles.

The wipers swiped away a light layer of snow just in time for me to see a black blur run in front of my truck. I slammed on my brakes.

The unmarked cruiser behind me slid sideways up onto the curb. BeBe jumped up, looked around, and started barking at the critter running through Mrs. Daasch's side yard.

A knock at the window startled me. I powered it down.

"Why the hell is there a turkey on the loose in the neighborhood?" Lewy wanted to know.

"Running for his life, probably," I shouted over BeBe's raucous barking.

Just like Kit? I wondered.

Out of the corner of my eye I saw a woman close my front door, get into her car. I blinked twice.

"Something wrong?" Lewy asked, following my gaze. "Ah."

Was that pity I saw in his eyes? Well, I didn't want it.

I shook my head, loosened my grip on the steering wheel. "Nothing's wrong. Not at all."

Out of all the people I expected to see, she wasn't one of them. And I just had to wonder what Ginger Ho, er, Ginger Barlow, was doing at my house.

Three

I parked behind Tam's Cabriolet, took a solid hold of BeBe's collar for fear she'd take off on a turkey hunt, and made my way up slippery front porch steps.

The walls to my house were notoriously thin, and I could hear the conversation inside without much trouble.

"What if he did it?" I recognized the voice of Jeff Dannon, one of my part-time employees. He was fairly new so I didn't hold his doubts against him. If he'd known Kit for any length of time, then he'd realize how ridiculous that notion was.

"Ach. He didn't." That from Brickhouse. She loved Kit almost as much as I did.

I hated that we had something in common.

"Who do you think did it?" It was the overeager voice of my neighbor, Mr. Cabrera. He loved gossip more than anyone I knew. He was fishing for speculation, and Tam bit.

"I never liked Daisy," she said. "And I can't be the only one."

"Did you ever meet her, *chérie*?" my mother asked Tam. The use of *chérie*, her signature endearment, was a dead giveaway.

"Well, no. But I didn't have to."

Brickhouse clucked. "Me either."

"So, who'd want to off her?" Mr. Cabrera pressed. He was a man on a mission for tidbits for the weekly neighborhood poker game. It used to be cribbage, but my stepson Riley had hooked Mr. Cabrera on Texas Hold 'Em over the summer, and the neighborhood hasn't been the same since.

"Maybe she had a new boyfriend." That from Mrs. Daasch, my neighbor two houses down.

"Or someone from that business of hers?" Jean-Claude Reaux, one of my full-time employees, said.

"Right, because those holistic types are so dangerous," Tam snipped.

"Hmmph. You never know," Jean-Claude said.

Jean-Claude was right. None of them knew about Daisy's freelance work—providing medicinal marijuana to those in need.

And although one would think peddling medicinal marijuana wouldn't be all that dangerous, Daisy had to have a supplier. Then there was the thought that maybe she didn't just sell to the sick . . .

And then there was the little problem of all those white pills. I had a feeling they weren't aspirin.

I suddenly recalled a conversation I'd overheard between Kit and Daisy last month.

"What you're doing is dangerous," Kit had said. "I'm worried about you."

And in light of what happened today, I couldn't shake her response: "Sometimes we have to do things to protect those we love."

I shuddered, unsure whether it was from the cold or from the memory. What had Daisy meant? And what had she been doing that was so dangerous?

As I reached for the door handle, I heard a voice from inside that made my stomach sink.

"You all can speculate as much as you want," he said, "but you have to accept the fact that Kit may be guilty. And in fact, probably is."

The voice explained why Ginger had been there, but not why she left without him.

I shoved the door open. My gaze skimmed past Mrs. Daasch, Brickhouse, Mr. Cabrera, my mother, Jeff Dannon, Tam, Jean-Claude, and Shay Oshwalter, to land on Kevin Quinn.

My ex.

I glared. Luckily, he looked deathly pale, so I withheld marching over to him and slapping him upside the head.

Guilty, my ass.

My mother was the first to break the silence. "Close the door, *chérie*, it's freezing!"

Then everyone spoke at once, throwing questions at me left and right.

BeBe pranced, working herself into a frenzy. I let go of her collar before she broke my arm. She took off, searching every corner of the room, stopping extra long to sniff at the duffel bag in the corner, where Kit kept most of his clothes. BeBe went from person to person. Finally, she must have realized Kit wasn't in the room and flopped down on the floor next to a suitcase.

A suitcase I didn't recognize.

But before I could question its ownership, the TV caught my attention. The sound was muted, but I could imagine what the anchor was saying as a picture of Kit flashed on the screen. It was his mug shot from years ago when he'd been arrested for indecent exposure after streaking across the fifty yard line at a Miami University football game.

Great. Now the public would think he was guilty too. Who was going to look beyond the mug shot and past mistakes to see the man he'd become?

Before everyone started foaming at the mouth, I told them everything I knew, right down to the aromatherapy scents in Daisy's treatment room.

Well, okay, I didn't mention a thing about the drugs. Not the marijuana, not the pills. I wasn't sure who I was trying to protect: Kit or Daisy.

Satisfied, most cleared out. Jean-Claude, Shay, and Jeff left first, worried about the roads. Tam wasn't far behind, especially after Ian called, worried about her driving in the bad weather.

Could Ian possibly help on this case at all? He might have information about Daisy selling drugs on a major level. As a former FBI agent and current DEA agent, he'd have connections.

I was reluctant to ask for help, though, knowing how busy he was these days. Kevin had been working undercover for him in a top secret sting operation when he was shot, and the investigation was still going on, taking up most of Ian's time.

But those pills might be a possible lead . . . I decided to call him later. I'd do everything possible to help prove Kit's innocence.

The neighbors were still gathered around, so I had to ask. "Anyone know anything about a wild turkey running through the neighborhood?"

After they stopped laughing, I convinced them I was serious.

"Not a thing, Miz Quinn," Mr. Cabrera said, gathering up his coat. He looped a scarf around his neck. It was forest green with white polar bears printed on it. "Lucky fella that he got away, with Thanksgiving being next week and all. Especially since so many in the neighborhood can barely afford a frozen one."

Sadly, it was true. The majority of the Mill's residents lived on social security. It left little for the extras in life. Those who did have extra usually made up the difference by having large neighborhood feasts or preparing baskets and care packages. It was a great neighborhood, one I was proud to live in.

Mrs. Daasch slipped a shawl over her shoulders. "Think we should call animal control?"

Mr. Cabrera waved the notion away. "I'll wrangle the fella up."

I held in a laugh, imagining Mr. Cabrera with a lasso and a ten gallon hat.

Brickhouse gathered up her wrap and opened the front door. Anxiety filled her icy blue eyes. "If you hear anything, call."

It was an order, but I didn't take offense.

She added, "You want the schnitzel to come with us?"

I glanced at BeBe, aka the schnitzel. Brickhouse was the only person to call her that. Thank goodness. "Sure." BeBe could probably use the change of pace. "I'll get her later."

The house was nearly empty as Mr. Cabrera, Brickhouse, and BeBe stepped out into the blowing snow. Darkness fell quickly along with the temperatures, casting the street into eerie shadows.

Riley walked in the front door just as my father emerged from the kitchen. I hadn't even known he was there. Maria, I'd learned, had gone skiing with her husband Nate for the weekend, but still planned on being at Thanksgiving dinner for the Big Day.

Shaking the snow from his hair, Riley didn't bother with a hello. Hmmph. He'd just turned sixteen and knew how to work my last nerve.

My mother fussed over him, taking his sweatshirt (since he refused to wear a coat) and offering him cocoa, which he turned down.

My first thought was that it was times like these when I could tell he wasn't my biological child. Turning down cocoa? Insanity.

My second thought was that my mother hadn't offered me any.

Hmmph.

"Everyone gone?" my dad asked, kissing my cheek. He smelled of cinnamon and vanilla, as usual.

I looked around. My mother, my father, Riley, Kevin.

One of these things definitely didn't belong here.

"Almost." I glanced at Kevin.

My dad gave me a quick hug. "I'm going to head out. I

have classes tomorrow and need my beauty sleep." He'd recently foregone retirement in favor of teaching at a local community college. No doubt to get away from my mother, who tended to smother. All in the name of love, of course.

"Drive safely," I said.

"I will."

He opened the front door, and I waited for my mother to follow.

She didn't budge.

To me, my father said, "Good luck," and ducked out.

My gaze snapped to my mother. "Luck? Why would I need luck?" I asked. "And shouldn't you be going too?"

"It's like this, *chérie* . . . "

It was never a good sign when sentences began that way.

Kevin grinned. "I'm moving in."

My head spun. "I need a drink, a snack, and a seat. It doesn't have to be in that order."

My mother led me to a large comfy chair, sat me down.

"Is that my pillow?" I asked Kevin. It was propped behind his back. "And my throw?"

"Very comfy. Is this down?" His green eyes sparkled as he fluffed the pillow, obviously toying with me.

Okay, on one hand I was glad to see he was doing better. On the other, I wanted to kill him, to put my pillow over his face and suffocate the smile from his lips.

"Cocoa?" my mother asked me.

It made me feel slightly better to finally be offered. I nodded, and she hurried to the kitchen.

Riley sat on the edge of the couch, near his father's legs. "I can explain."

I looked between the two of them, amazed by their resemblance. Riley had the same shape face, the same hair, the same build. He had his mother's eyes, though, a bright blue. Leah Quinn had died years before I met Kevin, in a mysterious accident I knew nothing about. And recently

I'd come to the conclusion that her death was none of my business, no matter how curious I was about it.

"Okay," I said to Riley. "Explain."

My mother brought me a hot chocolate. She must have had milk warming on the stove because she was back in a flash, sitting on the edge of the coffee table, smack dab in between Kevin and me.

I had a sudden flashback to my childhood, where she'd do the same when my brother Peter and I would go at it, or when I tried to shake some sense into my sister Maria.

"Now, Nina," she said, "this is temporary."

I sipped at the cocoa. No one made it like my mother. Just the right blend of chocolate, milk, and whipped cream. The mug warmed my hands, but the rest of me still felt cold. "Define temporary."

Riley shifted on the couch. His cheeks were still red from the cold. He'd probably been at Mrs. Greeble's. He'd been spending a lot of time there since starting work for her over the summer as a handyman. It warmed my heart, since as far as I knew, she had no other family in the area.

"A few days. Maybe a week," he mumbled.

"A week? Uh-uh. No way." Bobby's whole family was coming for Thanksgiving in six days. A week wasn't happening.

"He doesn't have anywhere else to go. I'm all he has left, and he needs my help," Riley said, his eyes wide, his voice cracking with emotion.

Jeez. The heavy guns right away? It wasn't fair. "Why not stay in the hospital another few days?" I asked Kevin.

"Because I was going crazy in there."

A small price to pay, in my opinion.

"Nina, please," Riley said softly.

I closed my eyes. Oh, Lord. I could deny Kevin in a heartbeat, but Riley? I felt myself caving, and latched onto my last hope. "Where's Ginger?"

Seemed to me Kevin and I were past the whole "in sickness and in health" vow. My turn was up. It was hers now. I didn't care if they were married or not—some things were just understood.

Like your lying, cheating ex-husband's postmedical care should be handled by his current bimbo.

Simple.

The microwave dinged, and my mother jumped up. Her lustrous blonde bob shimmered in the dim lighting, swaying in time with her footsteps. "Riley, come help me."

"But—" he protested.

"Come," she said sternly.

Once they were in the kitchen I looked at Kevin. "Ginger?" I prodded.

"Does it matter?" Kevin asked, wiggling his eyebrows. "Aren't you happy to have me here? Haven't you missed me?"

At my look, he laughed, then suddenly paled, grabbing at his chest. Fear pushed me from my seat to the edge of the couch.

"Are you okay?" My hand touched his leg and heat radiated into my palm. I yanked it back.

Pain contorted his grin into a grimace. "I knew you cared."

I thought about pouring my cocoa over his head, but didn't want to waste the chocolate on him.

Truth was, I did care.

"She's on her way to the airport, home to Wyoming. Her mother suddenly took ill this morning and wanted her to be there."

Of course, he couldn't go with her. He wasn't well enough to travel yet.

Great.

My mother reappeared a second later with a plate of mini pizza bagels. Pepperoni and sausage—mine and Riley's favorite. He had one in each hand.

Sighing, I forced myself to bite a bagel, though my appetite had suddenly vanished.

"I told Ginger to go," Kevin said. "She didn't want to leave me here."

That made two of us.

I looked at my mom. "How do you factor in?"

Riley sat on the arm of the couch. "I asked for Grandma Cel's help."

Ah, this made sense. My mother wouldn't have been able to say no to Riley either.

"Plus, you know me, *chérie*, I cannot turn down a soul in need."

Despite the fact that she still hadn't forgiven Kevin for cheating on me. I halfheartedly wondered if she'd planned to inflict any additional pain on him while she was here.

A girl could hope.

My mother folded her hands on her lap. "I'm here to change his dressings, *chérie*, and make sure he takes his medicine. You won't have to do a thing."

Outside, snow fell steadily. Across the street, Bobby's house was still dark.

I prayed Kit was warm.

"Well?" Riley asked, looking hopeful. "Can Dad stay?"

I looked at Riley, then Kevin. "All right. You can stay."

I hoped I wouldn't regret my decision.

Four

I shivered. My down vest was no match against the freezing cold temps and blowing snow. But I'd had to get out of the house, and Mr. Cabrera's gazebo seemed the perfect place to hunker down for a few minutes to call Ana and fill her in on the latest happenings.

She reacted much the way I anticipated she would.

"I should come home. I'm coming home. I'm taking the next flight. Mom," Ana shouted, "call the airlines!"

"Stop!" I said. "There's nothing you can do here."

"I can help look. Oh my God. I can't believe this is happening. I just saw Kit last night when he drove me to the airport. Oh."

"Oh what?"

"After dropping me off, he said he was on his way to see Daisy."

"Do you know why?"

"No, he wouldn't say."

"The police are trying to paint him as a jealous boyfriend."

She scoffed. "Hardly. He was over Daisy."

My fingers were losing feeling. "And how do you know that?"

There was a long silence.

Too long.

"He told me," she said.

"Ana . . . "

"What? He told me. We had a nice talk in the car on the way to the airport."

Something was definitely up. Eventually, I'd get it out of her. She wasn't one to keep secrets.

I kept an eye on Bobby's house, ready to sprint over there the minute his garage door opened.

"This isn't good, Nina. A six-foot-five brick wall with a skull tattoo on his head? And let's not forget the eyeliner. Where's someone like that supposed to hide? He's easily the most recognizable fugitive in the state."

"You're not making me feel better."

"I'm coming home."

My cell phone felt like an ice cube under my knit hat. "There's nothing you can do here, Ana."

The blinds were open in the back of Mr. Cabrera's house. I could see him standing in his dining room, fussing with a cardboard box. No doubt he was plotting his great turkey capture.

"There's got to be something. We can't let the police track him down, just to shoot first and ask questions later. Who's leading the case?"

"Darren Zalewski and Joe Nickerson."

"Old *Dickerson*?" Ana gasped. "Isn't he dead yet?"

I laughed. "I've missed you."

"I've only been gone one day."

"It's long enough."

"I should come home!"

"There's no—"

She cut me off. "Yeah, yeah." Softly, she then said, "I'm worried, Nina. I don't have much faith in the Freedom PD. Not after all the department's been through lately."

Can't say I blamed her. The department had been having troubles since last spring, and had been investigated by Internal Affairs, but nothing had come of it. The chief ended up looking like a fool, as did the prosecutor. The matter was dropped, but the department was still shaken and rumors persisted. Kevin laughed them off, and I thought if anyone had knowledge of what was going on, it would be him.

So I tried to have faith. Really, I did. But so far I hadn't been given much hope. I tried to reassure Ana, but she wasn't having any of it, so I decided to change the subject. "Oh," I said.

"What? What do I hear in that 'Oh'?"

"Kevin's staying with me for the next week."

"Oh!"

"Yeah. Recuperating." I filled her in.

"Now I've got to come home."

"Why?"

"Because I want to be there when you kill him."

My teeth chattered as I smiled. "I'll take pictures."

Abruptly, I straightened and pulled the phone away from my ear, listening closely. Something rustled the leaves. I covered the phone. "Is anyone there?" I asked loud enough to scare away any stalkers.

No one answered.

"Kit?" I whispered.

I crept out of the gazebo and toward the line of trees that bordered the back of the property.

"Kit?" I whispered again.

I heard muffled squawking and realized it was Ana.

"Is Kit there?" Her voice rose. "I heard you calling his name."

"I don't know," I whispered. "I heard something in the woods behind the house."

"Are you outside?"

"Yes."

"Isn't it about ten below with blizzard conditions?"

"Your point?"

"Why aren't you inside?"

I crept on tiptoes. My feet sank into ankle deep snow with each step. "Weren't you listening when I explained about Kevin?"

"Oh, that's right."

"Kit!" I called out again.

Something rustled in the brush, and all at once I wished I'd brought a flashlight.

"Do you see him?"

I inched closer. "No." Pulling back a branch of a sparse Norwood pine, I found myself staring upward into two dark beady eyes.

"Eeeee!" I screamed, and took off running from the turkey I'd found roosting in the tree.

He didn't appear happy to see me either.

A loud *turk-turk-turk* noise filled the air, and the rustling of feathers followed close behind me as he chased me through my yard.

It was the turkey escapee I'd seen earlier, running through the neighborhood.

And he was mad.

The turkey flapped his wings, fanned his tail, and chased me with a vigor I didn't know turkeys possessed.

"Eeeee!"

Mr. Cabrera's back door burst open and he flew out, cardboard box in hands. "Corner him, Miz Quinn, corner him!" he yelled at me.

BeBe chased after Mr. Cabrera, barking up a storm. Until she sniffed the air. Suddenly, she made a U-turn, tucked her tail and barreled back into the house.

Can't say I blamed her.

My back lights flashed on just as Lewy and Joe sprinted around the corner of the house, guns drawn.

"Don't shoot!" I cried.

Mr. Cabrera circled me as another turkey, a smaller one, wobbled out from behind the gazebo and joined in the fray, except this one clucked instead of turked.

"Holy Moses!" Mr. Cabrera shrieked. "There're two of them!"

Two! There were two turkeys! Where were they coming from, and how many friends did they have hiding in the woods?

"Hold still!" Joe shouted. "I'll shoot 'em."

"You'll do no such thing!" Mrs. Krauss yelled from the doorway of Mr. Cabrera's house. "I'll have your badge! There are laws against animal cruelty!"

I kept running, the bird chasing me, half running, half flying, wings flapping. Thank goodness my personal trainer, Duke, had gotten me into some semblance of shape.

The smaller turkey started after Mr. Cabrera, who threw the box into the air and beelined for his back door.

Lewy apparently found the whole situation hysterical until the big turkey turned on him.

"Run!" I yelled. Snow filled my Keds as I headed for my back door. Kevin and my mother stood on the back step, laughing so hard they had tears in their eyes.

Then I saw it.

Salvation.

The lights were on across the street.

"Gobble gobble," Kevin singsonged as I ran past him and across the street. "Or should it be bawk bawk?" he shouted after me, barely able to get the words out because he was laughing so hard.

I wasn't amused.

Dashing up the front steps, I pulled open Bobby's front door, stepped in, and slammed it closed.

My phone rang. Sometime during the ruckus, I must've hung up on Ana. I answered it with a terse, "I'm fine. I'll call you back," and snapped it closed.

Bobby came out of the kitchen, all six feet of blondheaded hunkiness, took one look at me, marched over, pulled me into his arms, and kissed me for all I was worth.

Which was quite a lot, it appeared.

"Better?" he asked, pulling away. He tugged my hat off my head, shook the snow loose, and hung it on the door handle.

No longer cold at all, I said, "Much."

He looked out the window. Squinted. "Is that a turkey running down the street?"

I nodded. "Keep looking. There's probably another one right behind it."

He squinted some more. "Is that Kevin standing on your front porch, glaring in this direction?"

I peeked, then nodded.

"Long story?" he asked me.

I nodded again.

His blue eyes glistened with curiosity. "Do I need alcohol?"

I nodded. "Any chance we can combine that with the bubble portion of tonight's agenda?"

He kissed me again. "Every chance."

I awoke to sun streaming in my bedroom windows, the bright glare blinding. Rolling over, I came face-to-face with BeBe, who licked me hello. Mrs. Krauss must have brought her over after the fray last night. Thankfully, Riley knew how to care for BeBe better than any of us. He'd been Kit's shadow for the past month.

I bolted upright, suddenly wondering if he knew what had happened with Daisy. My guess was that he hadn't known yesterday afternoon when begging me to let Kevin stay, but that he probably knew now.

"Need to go out?" I asked BeBe.

Her tail thumped my feather bed, plumping it. I pulled on my robe, grabbed a pair of thermal socks, and followed her downstairs.

Kevin was still asleep on the sofa bed, wrapped in a down comforter. His cheeks glowed a cozy pink. His short dark hair stood on end, and stubble covered his angular jaw.

My first thought was how drop-dead gorgeous he was.

My second speculated on how soon he could leave.

Having him there wasn't good for my mental health, because I suspected a part of me would always love him and be attracted to him, no matter who else was in my life.

Like Bobby.

And that just wasn't fair. To any of us.

"Good morning, *chérie*," my mother called from the kitchen. Fully dressed and perfectly coiffed, she sat at the island, sipping tea while reading today's paper. "What time did you get in?"

"Late."

Her eyebrows waggled. "Have fun?"

I felt myself blushing.

She laughed. "Good. You need some fun in your life."

I peeked out the kitchen window, and my jaw dropped. Sunbeams danced across freshly fallen snow. I shaded my eyes against the bright light and noticed the plows hadn't been by yet.

I was homebound until they showed up.

"A foot," my mother cooed. She loved snow. "A new record! We'll have to make angels."

I smiled and nodded. There was no age limit on enjoying a snow day. There was something magical about it, about snow angels, and snowmen, and hot cocoa and a roaring fire.

BeBe's tail whumped the door frame leading into the laundry room.

"I'll take her," my mother said, pulling on a pair of galoshes I kept near the back door.

I pressed a button on the coffeepot, and it whirred to life. "Thanks. And be careful of wild turkeys."

Wrapping a scarf around her head, protecting her ears, she laughed. "That's not something I hear every day."

As my coffee percolated I crept back up the stairs and into Riley's room. He lay diagonally across the bed, his blankets pulled up under his chin. Looking remarkably like his dad, he slept peacefully. When he woke, he was going to be cranky that it was Saturday. There was nothing worse to a kid than having a snow day on a weekend.

On my way out the door I spotted a deck of cards next to the lava lamp on his desk. I poked around a little, snooping. Riley had been on a huge Texas Hold 'Em kick for the past couple of months, and I had my suspicions he wasn't just playing for fun.

He'd had a lot of extra money lately, and though he did do a fair amount of work for Mrs. Greeble, she, like a lot of the other residents in the Mill, was on a fixed income. She wouldn't have much money to spare.

Finding nothing out of the ordinary, I backtracked, closing Riley's door behind me.

In my room, I took a quick shower, towel-dried my hair, and slipped on a pair of jeans and a fleece pullover. I thought about makeup, but opted for moisturizer and lip balm instead.

Downstairs, I heard the back door slam and the *click-clack* of BeBe's paws on the kitchen floor. I think I even heard my mother call BeBe "schnitzel" as she poured kibble into the doggy dish. Brickhouse was obviously spending too much time in the neighborhood.

I made my bed as the scent of coffee carried up the stairs. Outside, I heard a car struggling through the snow, and I went to the window. A dark Ford sedan slowed to a stop in front of my house. Lewy and Joe were back.

Nothing like their presence to ruin the serenity of a beautiful day.

My gaze skipped over their car to the house across the street. The blinds were still closed.

It seemed silly to have come back home last night just to share a bed with my mother (who hogged covers), but I'd felt funny staying with Bobby.

Well, staying with Bobby when Kevin knew I was with Bobby.

Yep.

The sooner Kevin left, the better.

My cell phone rang. I checked the display, smiled.

"Baby, it's cold outside," Perry said. "You'd better bundle up. I'll be there in an hour."

I checked the window again. Lewy and Joe hadn't budged. And still no sign of the plows. "You do know there's a foot of snow on the ground?"

"Foot, shmoot. I have a four-by-four."

From the corner of my eye I spotted two turkeys waddle down the street as though they were taking a leisurely stroll, heads held high, tails fanned, and wings dragging. All down the block doors opened and people stepped onto their front porches to watch.

It *was* quite a sight.

"Where exactly are we going?" I asked, because personally, I didn't have a clue where to start.

"On a manhunt, sugar." He laughed.

"What's so funny?"

"A manhunt. Oooh, I just love saying that."

I laughed. "You're certifiable, you know that?"

"One hundred percent." He took a moment, detailed the plan he had, then asked, "Are you game?"

"There's probably a snow emergency in effect."

"And this isn't an emergency? Finding Kit?"

He had a point. "All right. I'm in." Exhaust puffed from the unmarked car's tailpipe. The two turkeys pecked around their tires. "Park down the block. I'll meet you there. And watch out for the turkeys."

I flipped the phone closed before Perry commented, and smiled. Perry and I would be tracking down Kit while Lewy and Joe sat out front with the turkeys—right where they belonged.

I just hoped Perry and I weren't headed on a wild goose chase.

Five

Sneaking out of the house had been fairly easy. I'd simply walked into the back hall with a load of laundry, turned on the washer, and slipped out the back door.

I'd left a note taped to the dryer that I'd be home soon. No need for my mother to worry—or to send out the FBI.

My feet left deep impressions in the snow as I cut through three backyards before reaching the corner, where Perry had his black Range Rover idling. Gray snow caked the undercarriage and wheel wells.

He threw open the passenger door, I jumped in, and he peeled out, as though he was Starsky and I was Hutch. Snow flew out behind us.

Perry fairly bounced in his seat. "I have to say, Nina, this is the most excited I've been in quite some time."

Drawing the seat belt over my shoulder, I smiled. "I'll be sure to let Mario know." The two had been together for just over a year.

He laughed, a loud, deep, infectious sound that made me smile wider. "Oh, he knows, sugar. He knows."

I wasn't worried for their relationship. They were perfectly matched. Perry's exuberance was the perfect foil to Mario's cool confidence.

"Now," he said, looking at me through a pair of lightly

tinted aviator sunglasses, "either my happy pills are too strong and I'm hallucinating, or I saw an actual turkey waddling down your street."

Adjusting the blower on the dash, I directed heat toward my frozen face. I laughed. "No need to adjust your medication. The Mill is apparently the new home of a pair of wild turkeys."

He sighed wistfully. "Too bad you're not referring to my kind of Wild Turkey."

I stole a glance at his face. "I thought you quit drinking."

"I did, but I miss it."

Times like these I could see why. Fortunately, Perry hadn't had a problem with alcohol—just the calories that came with it. He was on a diet and hoarding points for Thanksgiving dinner like a hungry squirrel gathering nuts for hibernation.

Five days. Thanksgiving was in five short days, and I hadn't even bought the turkey yet. Maybe the neighborhood's wild turkeys were a sign from above to get my act in gear. Twenty people were due at my house Thursday afternoon. The Big Day. The day my family was to meet Bobby's. Plus, I'd invited a few strays. Mario and Perry, Tam and Ian, Flash Leonard, several people from work, and of course Kit.

"No inside scoop on Kit?" Perry asked, slowly turning onto the northbound I-75 on ramp. Sparse traffic kept a steady pace, sloshing down the salt- and snow-covered highway.

I slipped on my sunglasses, the glare from the sun on the snow harsh. "Nothing." He'd simply vanished. Poof. Gone.

Perry glanced at me. "Have you been watching the news?"

I warmed my hands in front of the blower, started counting all the cars that had slid off the side of the road. Five minutes and I'd already seen three. "I've been trying not to."

According to the reports I had seen, the police weren't saying much. Daisy was shot to death, Kit was a person of interest, and it appeared that drugs might have been a factor in her death. One newscast mentioned a broken window at Heavenly Hope and how the perpetrator might have gained access that way.

Little did they know.

"Stupid bloodthirsty media." Perry's creamy skin glowed with good health, and his tawny hair lay hidden beneath a cream-colored cashmere stocking hat.

Usually I wasn't as jaded as Perry, but I couldn't help but agree with his assessment, especially since the media was going out of its way to make it seem that Kit was guilty until proven innocent.

"We need to think about this case rationally," he said.

"Are you saying I'm not rational?" I teased.

"Sugar, I'm surprised you're functioning. I know how you feel about Kit."

To me, Kit was another sibling. Nina, Maria, Peter . . . Kit. It tore me apart to think about all the what-ifs in light of Daisy's death.

Obviously trying to comfort me, Perry patted my hand. "Back to rational. Who would want Daisy dead? What are some motives?"

"Money, greed, betrayal, revenge. The list is endless."

"We know Kit didn't do her in, so someone out there did. We need to put her life under a microscope, talk to anyone and everyone who knew her. She had to have employees, right?"

"Heavenly Hope looked well-established. I would think so."

"They'd be a good place to start. Clients too. Do you think we can track any down?"

"I don't know. The master list was probably on her hard drive, and that was missing from her office. Maybe we can find a few through her employees."

"It's not much to go on," he said. "But it's a start."

It was more than the police were doing.

"Lord above, it would be nice if Kit's hiding out at his mom's, and we can get the whole story."

Again my mind went to the dark side. That he couldn't be at his mom's because whoever killed Daisy killed him too.

Think positive, Nina. Think positive.

It was hard. Very hard.

Dropping my head back against the seat, I wondered who could help if Kit's mom hadn't heard anything. One name jumped to the top of my list, and I made a mental note to give her a call.

Perry chattered about the snow, and Mario, and my hair, which he said needed retouching. I liked Perry. A lot. He was a lot of fun. But right now I missed Ana. She was my usual partner in crime. Plus, she would have brought hot chocolate.

"There's hot chocolate in the backseat," Perry said, as if reading my mind. "Godiva, mmmm."

I definitely agreed with his assessment, and decided maybe I didn't miss Ana so much after all.

After foraging for the thermos and pouring myself a capful of cocoa, I glanced in the side mirror. No one seemed to be following us.

Perry sipped from an insulated cup as I said, "I hope we're not wasting our time."

"Listen, sugar, imagine you're in trouble, possibly in danger. Where would you run to?"

Without a second thought I said, "Mom."

"Exactly. There's no place like home when you're in need."

Kit's mother lived two hours north of the Mill in a small town. Ash, population 2,000, was but a speck on my Ohio map. "His Hummer was in the parking lot at Heavenly Hope. How would he have gotten up to Ash?"

"Could he have had Daisy's car?" he asked.

I shook my head. "It was at her house."

"Maybe Mama Pipe drove down and picked him up. It would be nice if we could get our hands on his cell phone records."

His cell phone had been found in his Hummer, but that didn't mean he hadn't made a call before he took off.

Or was taken out.

I couldn't allow myself to think that way. I needed a clear head, not one filled with anxiety. With a shaky hand, I reached for the thermos for a second shot of cocoa.

"I think he's too smart to have used his cell phone," I said. "Too easy to track with the GPS in his phone." Hope buoyed. "That might be why he left it behind."

I liked that conclusion better than the one my morbid mind had jumped to.

"He is a smart cookie, that Kit. You have to remember, sugar, that he's been around the block a time or two. He can take care of himself."

Perry was right. But it was hard not to worry.

His cell phone rang, a rousing rendition of the "William Tell Overture." He looked at the readout and cheerily answered the call.

After a second his smile faded. "Maybe," he said. Then added, "What did you tell them?"

I could vaguely hear Mario's smooth voice crackling through the phone. I looked out the window. The car count was up to eight as I spotted a blue sedan in a snow bank on the side of the highway.

"All right, thanks. I will. Buh-bye."

Perry tucked his cell phone into his cup holder and looked over at me. "You've apparently upset some people."

I could make a list. "Anyone specific?"

"Two detectives just called Mario, looking for you."

Lewy and Joe, no doubt. "What did Mario tell them?"

"He said you were with me on a road trip to Indiana to see my aunt, but we were incommunicado for the next four hours. And that hunky ex of yours called too."

Kevin? "Why?"

"Same deal. Except he didn't believe Mario."

"He's smart that way. Detectives Zalewski and Nickerson are probably headed to Indiana right about now. Out to track us down."

"Why, sugar?" He peered at me.

"Why what?"

"Why are they watching you so closely? They don't suspect you, do they?"

I shook my head. "They're hoping I lead them right to Kit."

He smiled. It lit his whole face. "Then let's have some fun with them."

Shifting in my seat, I said, "What do you have in mind?"

We'd driven almost ninety minutes before we had the plan in place. By the time we pulled up to Kit's mother's house, a well-kept modest ranch, I had called Tam and set the plan in motion.

There were two cars in the Pipe driveway. I recognized neither one. Snow crunched beneath my Timberlands as Perry and I made our way to the front door.

"What have you got?" I asked.

"Bundt cake," he said, holding up a pretty cake plate he'd pulled out of the backseat. "Made it myself."

I hadn't thought to bring anything. But then again, I hadn't been thinking too well since finding Daisy's body.

The doorbell echoed.

Shivering, I tried to keep warm by moving from foot to foot.

"Stop," Perry ordered. "You're making me motion sick."

The door flew open, and I looked into the teary eyes of Madelyn Pipe, Kit's mom. "Nina!" she cried, tugging me into a hug. She was a sturdy woman, maybe five-foot-eight, two hundred pounds, with an enormous smile. Her chest heaved as she stepped back. "I'm so glad you're here," she said, not letting go of my hand.

"Maddie, this is Perry Owens," I said, introducing him. She smiled. "I recognize you from that show!"

Perry and I groaned. We both wanted to forget the reality show we'd done.

"Come in, come in," she said. "I'm sorry the place is a mess. I haven't been able to think straight since I heard the news."

My condition was apparently contagious. "Don't worry about it, Maddie."

Perry handed her the bundt cake. "I made it myself."

Maddie smiled, but her eyes still looked sad. "Perry, is that fresh coconut?" she asked in awe.

"Grated this morning!" Proud as a peacock, he and Maddie talked baking as if nothing untoward had happened and Perry and I dropped in all the time.

I stepped into the living room and froze as I spotted a clearly upset couple sitting on a comfortable looking ultra-suede sofa. "Hello," I stammered.

Maddie came up behind me, touched my shoulder. "Nina, Perry, this is Dill and Rose. Daisy's parents."

If there were ever a time I wanted to crawl under a rock and hide, this was it. I eyed the bottom of the sofa. I wouldn't fit, even now that I was leaner thanks to Duke's hardcore training.

What to say? Certainly not *Pleased to meet you*. "I, uh, I'm so sorry for your loss," I said. I shot a look to Perry. He looked sorrier for the position he was now in than for Daisy being dead.

"Me too," he said, minding his manners.

Rose Bedinghaus nodded. "Thank you."

Maddie set the cake on a glass-topped coffee table. "This here is Nina Quinn and Perry Owens. Nina is Kit's boss."

Dill's eyes widened. Rose gasped softly.

Maybe I could squeeze under that couch if I tried really hard . . .

"Sit, sit," Maddie offered, her cheeks bright red.

Perry took my arm and guided me into a side chair. It wasn't until I sat down that I realized how dizzy I'd been. Spots swam before my eyes, the kind you get if you stare at the sun for a second too long.

What did one say to the parents of the woman you just found dead the day before?

"Anyone hungry?" Perry asked, obviously trying to break the tension. "I'm sure Maddie and I can grab plates, forks, and some coffee."

Maddie looked like she was as eager to escape as Perry. "Coffee's good. I've got some in the kitchen. Perry, want to help? Kit bought me one of those newfangled grinders, and I can't figure it out."

"My specialty," he said. They fairly sprinted out of the room.

It struck me then that Maddie didn't seem too worried about Kit. Had she heard from him? Was he here? Hiding upstairs? I listened closely for creaks but didn't hear anything.

Finally, I forced myself to look at Daisy's parents. "I'm sorry. This is awkward."

Rose had the same color hair as Daisy, a lively red, except hers was cut short in a cute pixie style, while Daisy's had been long and flowing. Dill looked to be mid-sixties, with graying brown hair, a nicely trimmed beard and mustache. Both had bright blue eyes that swam with tears.

"Kit always spoke highly of you," Rose said. "I know how grateful he was that you let him stay with you this past month."

I leaned forward in my chair. "You were still in touch with Kit?"

"Some," Dill answered for his wife. "He'd become like a son to us over the last few years. Those ties are hard to break, lickety-split."

"I really am sorry," I said again. I couldn't imagine what it would be like to lose a child. I was a basket case when

Riley so much as got a paper cut, and he wasn't even my flesh and blood.

Rose's gaze didn't waver. "Did she look like she suffered?"

My stomach turned. "No," I said honestly. "There didn't appear to be a struggle. The only wound I could see was the shot to her chest, which had to have killed her instantly." I'd made up that last part, but felt the need to say it to ease their pain, if just a little.

Rose's breath caught. "Thank you for being honest."

Since I hadn't been—completely—I felt the sudden urge to study the intricacies of the wrought-iron coffee table base.

Dill shifted on the sofa. His dark brown blazer pulled taut against his shoulders as he leaned forward, steepling his fingers. "Do you think Kit did it?"

There was no hesitation on my part. "No."

Rose nodded. "We don't think so either. Kit isn't the violent type. I tried to tell the officers that, but they didn't seem to care."

A loud grinding noise came from the kitchen. The scent of fresh coffee filled the air. I inhaled, having recently become addicted to the brew.

"I have to admit," I said, "the circumstantial evidence is stacked against Kit. But everyone who knows him realizes he would never hurt anyone, let alone Daisy."

"Even though they broke up, he still loved her," Rose said with conviction.

"He did," I said. "More now as a friend, I think, but yes. He cared for her quite a bit."

Dill leaned back. "Too bad she didn't feel the same."

"Dill," Rose chastised.

"It's true," he said. "Or why would she take up with someone else and walk away from a man like Kit?"

Rose said softly, "We can't choose love."

Dill harrumphed.

I felt my eyes widen. Heat suffused my face. "Someone else?"

"You didn't know?" Dill asked me.

"No, I didn't."

Rose tried to soften the blow. "A few months ago she fell head over heels for a man she met through work."

Months? Plural? She and Kit had only been broken up for one month. "Do the police know this?"

"We told them. It just seemed to fuel their fire where Kit was concerned. Added motive, they said. A lover spurned."

"Have you met this man?"

"No, but I know his name is Kent Ingless. I saw it on her caller ID one day—that's probably the only reason we know about him. Daisy was very private. Kit knew," Rose added. "About Kent."

"He did?" He'd never said anything to me. Yet, why would he?

"Kit met him once while at Heavenly Hope helping Daisy," Maddie said, coming in from the kitchen, carrying a tray filled with steaming mugs and colorful plates.

"Kit was helping her?" I asked, thoroughly confused.

Maddie perched on a love seat. She sliced through the bundt cake. "With her business."

Rose took a proffered plate. "She'd been having some trouble."

Perry sat across from me in a matching chair. Fork poised, he said, "Trouble?"

The drugs. It had to be. How much did Daisy's parents know?

Dill waved off the cake. "We're not sure with what. We're hoping the police can figure it out. All I know is that Daisy had been grateful for Kit's help. And that she was hoping they'd be able to stay friends."

"Did Daisy have many employees?" I asked, hoping to get some names.

"No," Rose said, taking a bite of cake. "She had a partner, Randall Oh, an acupuncturist who studied old world herbal medicine. Between the two of them, they covered all the work."

"Not even a receptionist?"

Rose set her plate on her lap and reached for her mug. "Not even."

Interesting. Why not? If business was booming, why not add more employees?

Unless Daisy was going to great lengths to keep people out.

I remembered again about Kit being worried about Daisy's safety. Whatever danger she'd been in revolved around Heavenly Hope. That, I knew for sure. Was it simply the medicinal marijuana business? Or had there been something more? Something to do with those little white pills?

And just how involved was Kit?

Six

"I love that woman," Perry said. "I want her to be my mother."

The sun had disappeared behind thick clouds, leaving the sky a murky gray. Snowflakes fell.

"What's the matter, sugar? You're pouting."

Folding my arms over my chest, I said, "I just don't get it."

"Get what?"

"Why wouldn't Kit tell me about this other man in Daisy's life? Why not tell me he was helping her with Heavenly Hope?"

"Honestly? I don't know."

"You're a big help, Perry."

"Don't go getting snippy with me, young lady."

I smiled at his tone. "Sorry. I'm just confused. Did you learn anything from Maddie in the kitchen? She didn't seem too worried about Kit to me."

We'd stayed for two hours, and were able to spend an hour of that time alone with Maddie. If she knew anything at all, she didn't let it slip.

And much to our dismay, Kit hadn't made an appearance.

"Let's see. I learned her secret for making the best home-made apple pie. I learned she alphabetizes her spices. I learned—"

I cut him off. "I'm not amused. I'm a woman on the edge, Perry."

He laughed. "She told me she hasn't heard from him."

Shocked, I said, "You asked her outright?"

"I don't believe in beating around the bush, sugar."

I admired his gumption. "Do you believe her?"

"Not at all. She has this habit of licking her lips when she lies. I picked up on it right away when I asked about Kit."

"The police will check her phone records. They'll know."

"Not necessarily. If he called from a pay phone, then she just has to say someone called but it was the wrong number."

"Awfully coincidental."

"Maybe so, but there wouldn't be enough evidence to get her into trouble."

I wished she'd told us if Kit had called. Just to set my mind at ease. However, for the first time in a day and a half, I relaxed a bit. I was fairly sure Kit was okay. I didn't have a clue as to where he was or what kind of danger he'd placed himself in, but he was okay.

Now I just had to figure out a way to clear his name, because it was obvious to me the police had already tried and convicted him.

I had a couple of leads to follow. I needed to call Ian and ask about the pills I'd seen. I also wanted to find the new man in Daisy's life. And how much did Randall Oh know about Daisy's freelance work? And was he part of it?

"Can I borrow your phone again?" I asked. I'd left mine at home.

Without a word, Perry handed it over. His wipers pushed the snow from the windshield. Traffic on the highway had gone from three lanes to one.

Tam answered on the fourth ring. I could hear her daughter Niki cooing in the background.

"It's me again. I'm just checking in," I said.

"Any news?" Worry laced her voice.

I told her about our visit with Kit's mom. "I think Maddie knows where Kit is. She doesn't seem worried."

Tam let out a breath. "That's good news."

"How's everything there?"

She knew what I was asking. "Coby just crossed the Tennessee border. Harvey's right behind him."

Perry's plan, so far, was working perfectly. Soon, Lewy and Joe would be taking a long road trip.

Snow fell steadily. I spotted another car in a ditch on the side of the road. Number eleven. Thankfully, Perry was a great driver.

"As soon as they reach Atlanta, they're going to abandon Coby's TBS truck on the side of the road."

And Harvey would drive him back.

"Call me as soon as they're on the way back. I'll let the good detectives know a TBS truck is missing. Hopefully they'll think Kit took it and is on his way to warmer climes."

I could hear the smile in her voice. "Then they'll leave you alone."

"That's the hope."

"Serves them right."

I couldn't agree with her more.

By the time Perry turned down my street, the snow had stopped, the sun was peeking out from the clouds, and I was having second thoughts about sending Lewy and Joe on a wild goose chase.

It had to be a misdemeanor at the very least. If they weren't all that happy with me already, then what would they do if they found out I was obstructing justice?

Would I spend Thanksgiving in the clink? Actually, with the way my holiday was shaping up, the clink wasn't looking so bad.

I bet the jailhouse cooks already had their turkeys. I wouldn't have to worry about all the things that usually go wrong on Thanksgiving. Like the turkey not being fully defrosted. The potatoes having lots of black spots, the rolls being burned, the gravy lumpy.

The clink was looking up, in my opinion.

And I was rambling to myself—clearly a sign that I was stressed out.

I took a deep breath and decided to let things be. If I wanted to be free to track down the people in Daisy's life, then I needed to be rid of Lewy and Joe.

Hopefully, they wouldn't find out.

"I don't suppose you want to come in?" I asked Perry as he pulled to the curb in front of my house.

"As much as I want to meet the ex, I promised Mario I'd be home in time for dinner. He gets cranky when I'm late."

I leaned across the console, kissed his cheek. "Thanks for driving . . . and everything."

"Same time tomorrow?" he asked. We already had plans to track down Kent Ingless.

"Make it an hour earlier. I really need to do some grocery shopping tomorrow afternoon."

I hopped out of the car. There was no sign of Lewy and Joe, and I had to wonder if they had really gone to Indiana.

Part of me hoped they had, and part of me hoped they were smarter than to fall for a trick like that.

Because if they were smarter, then maybe they'd be able to find out who actually killed Daisy.

I opted to go in the back door through the laundry room so I wouldn't have to face Kevin right off the bat. Sometime during the day, someone—I assumed it was my mother—had moved the wash into the dryer. I unlaced my boots, set them on the mat to dry. I tiptoed out of the back hall and peeked into the kitchen.

All clear.

I was headed through the kitchen to the stairs and the safety of my bedroom when I heard Kevin's voice. He was on the phone.

"Don't worry," he was saying. He sat on the couch. There was a college football game on the TV screen, but the sound was down to a bare whisper. "I'm handling it. No, she doesn't. Not a clue."

I crept to the doorway, my curiosity piqued. Who was the she in question? Me? And what was he handling?

Kevin flipped the channel to another football game. "You don't have to worry, Ginger. It's not going to happen . . . Because I know." His voice rose in frustration. "Because I do."

Ginger. Ah. But what were they bickering about?

Kevin shifted on the couch. His voice grew tight, controlled. "There's no need for you to worry. I'm just staying here." He paused, listening. "No, it doesn't. She has her own life. Besides, she doesn't want me, remember?"

My heart thudded to a stop. Ginger was worried about Kevin and me? That was rich.

He let out a heavy breath. "We've been through this. Nina and I are over." He pushed a hand through his hair, sending dark spikes shooting upward. "You've got nothing to be jealous about." He scoffed. "Nice. Thanks for throwing that in my face."

I'd have given just about anything to hear her half of the conversation.

"I'm done," he said. "If you're so worried, come back. It's got to be better than sitting in the airport, waiting for the runways to open." He listened, then straightened. "Fine, it's probably better that way."

He pressed the End button on the phone and dropped it onto the couch. Fingering the remote, he turned off the TV and dropped his head back, groaning.

I couldn't let him see me standing here; that would be too awkward for words.

Slowly, I crept back, toward the back hall. The floor creaked. I froze as Kevin's head snapped up. As if in slow motion, he turned and looked my way.

Our eyes locked.

I could see torment in his, and I wasn't sure what he might be seeing in mine. Panic, guilt, remorse. Any number of things.

Before either of us could say a word, the doorbell rang. I sprinted over and pulled it open before the buzzer even finished sounding.

Lewy and Joe stood on the front porch. I was actually happy to see them. "Come in, come in," I urged. "Sit down. Would you like some coffee? Water? Tea? Cocoa. Let me take your coats."

Their eyes narrowed as I tugged at their boring beige trenches. Lewy looked between Kevin and me slowly. I smiled brightly. Kevin scowled.

"Water is good," Joe said. The look on his face clearly stated he thought I was a crazy woman.

I might just be.

"Water's fine," Lewy said.

"Good, good. I'll go get it." Rushing into the kitchen, I took my sweet time filling two glasses of water while trying to eavesdrop on the conversation in the living room.

I could only imagine.

I was just starting to wonder where my mother, Riley, and BeBe were when I saw them out the back window building a snowman. 'Least, my mother and Riley were trying, and BeBe was trying to knock it down. She might have been afraid of turkeys, but when it came to snowmen, she was a fierce opponent.

Slowly, I walked back into the living room, passed Joe and Lewy their water.

Kevin could fend for himself.

"Well, gentlemen. It was nice seeing you again." I headed toward the stairs.

"Wait." Kevin glared at me. "Care to tell me where you snuck off to today?"

I paused on the first step. "Nope."

"If you're interfering with an investigation, Nina . . . "

"Who said I'm 'interfering'?"

Kevin jabbed a finger in the air. "So you *were* snooping!"

"Snooping is such a negative term." I inched onto the second step. Only eleven more to go.

Kevin growled. "I can't protect you this time, Nina. Stay out of it. Lewy and Joe won't hesitate to lock you up."

They both nodded.

Despite my earlier thoughts about the clink, I didn't want to go there. I backed down a step, my temper rising. "Did you know Daisy's business was in trouble? Kit was trying to help her. Or about how she sold therapeutic marijuana? Or about her new boyfriend? Has any of this been investigated?"

"It's being looked into," Lewy said.

I didn't believe him for a moment.

"We don't know what happened, Nina," Kevin said. "You have to accept that Kit may be responsible. He could have been angry that Daisy was in love with another man. Love is a powerful motive."

I looked between the three of them. "Is this really how it's going to be? Railroad Kit? Use him as a scapegoat? Why? To make the department look good after all the bad publicity? To get a quick conviction for the prosecutor?" I threw my hands in the air. "Is this just another example of the good old boys covering for each other? You make me sick."

I folded my arms over my chest. I'd worked myself into quite a tizzy and could feel my heart thumping against my wrist.

Lewy held up his hands. "Hey, now. Can I have a word with you? In private?"

"You better go outside," Kevin said. He shot me a look. "There's no such thing as privacy in here."

He was referring to the phone call.

"Feel free," I said to him, "to hobble on back to your own house."

"Nina?" Lewy said. His tone had softened, and he looked

like the Lewy I used to know, the one who came over every now and again with his family for a barbecue.

It was a nice try, but I wasn't falling for it. "No," I said. "Not without a lawyer."

I didn't wait for a response as I rushed to the back hall, pulled open the back door, and slammed it behind me.

Seven

The sun had begun sinking into the western horizon. Wind whipped between Mr. Cabrera's and my yard, nearly cutting me in two with cold. A coat would have been nice. But there was no way I was going back for one. Stubborn, yes, but I didn't want to face Kevin.

From the backyard, I could hear my mother singing in French, and Riley moaning about it. BeBe barked happily.

I headed in their direction to make snow angels until a loud scream echoed down the street.

My mother and Riley came running. "Who's that?" my mother asked me as we all jogged toward the road.

Across the road Flash Leonard scrambled out of his house too, obviously in search of the screamer.

"I'm not sure," I said.

The screams picked up in intensity and were laced with swearing. They came from Miss Maisie's front yard. We took off down the street, Riley sprinting ahead.

The wind chilled me to the bone. My teeth chattered. "Where's BeBe?"

"Tied up in the backyard. I think she's falling in love with the snowman. She keeps licking its face."

For some reason, I wasn't the least bit surprised.

Miss Maisie lived five houses down, across the street, next door to Mrs. Greeble. Maisie had been widowed since

1971 and refused to remarry. We found her on her front porch. She had something cornered under the porch swing, and her language made me blush.

Riley's mouth dropped open in shock.

"Like you've never heard those words before," I said to him.

"Not coming from an eighty-year-old woman!"

Actually, I'd never heard them come from an eighty-year-old woman either.

"Maisie!" Flash bellowed. "What in God's good name are you screeching about?"

Miss Maisie straightened and looked over her shoulder at us. A small delicate hand went to her lips, covering them. Color burned her cheeks, though from the cold or embarrassment, I wasn't sure.

As soon as she backed away from the swing, a small white blur ran out.

My mother squealed. Miss Maisie swung her broom this way and that, nearly knocking Riley clear off the steps. "Get him!" she yelled.

The "him" in question was a snow white rooster. It flapped its wings and ran in circles, while Miss Maisie tried to sweep it into oblivion.

"Mercy me!" my mother shouted.

Riley looked to be in complete and utter shock, his eyes wide, his mouth open. Either that or he'd seen his life flash before his eyes when the broom came at him again.

"Grab it!" Miss Maisie yelled at me.

I spun around as the rooster ran circles around my feet. I bent down and reached out, but the rooster ran right through my legs—still free as, well, a bird.

"Why didn't you grab him, Nina?" Flash asked me.

"I can't feel my hands!"

"Where's your coat?" he asked me.

"Long story, Flash."

"Well, I can't catch him! Not with my arthritis. Riley?"

Riley sprang into action, chasing the bird around the

yard. It was my mother, however, who reached down and plucked the rooster from the ground, holding it firmly in the crook of her arm.

I wasn't sure who looked more surprised, me or the rooster, who I immediately named Gregory Peck. He was a handsome little guy.

Winded, Riley dropped onto Miss Maisie's bottom step. "Grandma Cel, where'd you learn to do that?"

"I grew up on a farm, *chérie*."

My mouth dropped open and I spoke around my chattering teeth. "You grew up on a farm? How come I didn't know this?"

My mother shrugged.

Argh.

Mr. Cabrera came jogging up, not wanting to miss out on the action. "A rooster!"

"It's becoming an epidemic," Miss Maisie stated, banging her broom against the wooden floorboards of her porch. "A poultry plague."

I saw Riley ease away.

"It's true," Flash said. "First the turkeys, then a rooster?"

"Is someone trying to get rid of us?" Miss Maisie asked, her dark eyes wide with fear.

I thought it both a bit dramatic and paranoid of her, but didn't want to upset her by saying so. "How?" I asked.

"I was just watching a news story the other day about the bird flu! These birds could be contaminated. Someone probably brought them to the Mill to infect us so they could clear the neighborhood of the old riffraff. Developers would love this land to build spiffy new condos."

Immediately, my mother dropped the rooster. It took off, running zigzag across Miss Maisie's yard.

"Now, Maisie," Flash began, apparently having no qualms against upsetting the woman. "That's silly."

I crossed my arms and tucked my hands into my armpits to keep my fingers from getting frostbitten. "They're not contaminated," I said. "There's been no bird flu reported in the U.S. yet."

"Then you explain it," Miss Maisie demanded.

Two turkeys. One terrified rooster. I had no explanation whatsoever.

"That's what I thought," she snapped. "Someone has to catch that rooster so we can get it tested."

No one budged.

Miss Maisie took the tearful approach. "Our lives could be at stake!"

My mother nudged me. "Go get the rooster, *chérie*."

"Oh, sacrifice your favorite child."

She arched an eyebrow. "Nonsense. You're the only one fast enough. You've been working out."

I looked at Riley.

"He's but a child, *chérie*!"

Gritting my teeth, I went after the rooster. My mother called out tips. "Grab him around the middle, Nina! Catching roosters is in your genes. You should have no problems."

I was cold. I was upset about Kit. I was mad at Kevin. The last thing I wanted to be doing was catching a runaway rooster that might or might not be carrying the bird flu.

And, to top it all off, I had problems. It seemed Gregory Peck didn't want to be caught. He led me all around the yard, and by the time I grabbed him by his skinny little leg and was able to get my hands around his middle, the clink was looking good again.

"Now what?" I asked once I caught the bird.

No one had an answer.

"Chérie, why are your lips blue?"

Argh!

"Here." I shoved the bird at Mr. Cabrera. "Put him in your garage. I'll call Animal Control. I'm going home."

"There's no need to be crabby, Miz Quinn." Gregory Peck flapped his wings. "Whoa, whoa," Mr. Cabrera said to the rooster, trying to calm it as though it was a horse.

With that image in my head, I hurried home. I walked in the front door and closed it behind me, tempted to lock it. Kevin was on the phone. Lewy and Joe were sitting on my sofa, both sipping coffee from my favorite *Wizard of Oz* mugs.

I froze. I'd been hoping they would be long gone.

"You don't smell so good," Joe said, sniffing.

I looked down at myself. Gregory Peck had left a calling card behind—on my shirt.

"What are you two still doing here?" Glancing out the window, I saw their car. It sat at the curb—I'd completely overlooked it.

Joe leaned forward. "We'd like to know where you were this morning, Nina."

"Out," I said.

"Out isn't going to cut it." Lewy sipped his coffee.

"I went for a ride with a friend."

"Where?"

"We were headed for Indiana, but got lost, then the roads were so bad we decided to turn around."

I was a great fibber.

"You're good, Nina," Joe intoned melodramatically, "but we're better. Just remember that."

I shivered, but not from his words. I was frozen to the bone. Truthfully, the pair didn't scare me in the least. I thought maybe Gregory Peck had more brains than the two of them combined.

"If we find out you've been aiding and abetting . . . "

"Yeah, yeah." I motioned to the phone. "Is that for me?"

Kevin handed it over. "It's Tam," he said.

I took the call.

"He's stubborn," Tam said once I was on the line. "He wouldn't listen to a word I said about Kit."

"I had to live with that for seven years." I smiled at Kevin, and he growled. He'd been doing that a lot lately. So much for being grateful for my hospitality. "What's up?" I asked Tam.

Clearing her throat, she said, "I hate to be the bearer of bad news, but one of the TBS trucks is missing."

She went on to tell me the story just as we'd rehearsed. I made appropriately distressed noises where I was supposed to. The whole act was just in case the phone lines were tapped—something I wouldn't put past the two sitting on my couch.

I hung up and faced the three men who'd like nothing better than to see Kit in jail.

"What's going on?" Kevin asked.

"Nothing," I hedged, playing my part really well.

"We have ways of finding out if you're lying," Joe said.

Well, that answered the question of the phones being tapped.

"Oh, all right. One of my TBS trucks is missing from the lot at work. It was there yesterday and wasn't there today."

Lewy jumped up, walked to the corner of the room and made a call from his cell phone. It took me much effort not to smile.

I ducked into the kitchen and came out with the phone book. "Who are you calling?" Joe asked.

"None of your business."

"Everything you do is my business, Nina," he answered. Amazingly, he didn't sound happy about it either.

"I'm aware," I said, grumpy.

I found the number for the Animal Control office and called, leaving a message on their machine.

"A rooster?" Kevin asked once I hung up.

"He's quite handsome."

"Testy, I bet," Joe said. "Those roosters always are."

Kevin and I looked at him.

"Grew up on a farm," he mumbled, draining the last of his coffee.

"Shouldn't you two be leaving now?" I asked Joe.

"We thought we'd just hang around for a while longer," Lewy said after finishing his call.

I could have argued about civil liberties and warrants and such, but decided to take an easier way out. "Fine by me. I'm going to go take a shower." I started up the stairs, then stopped. "Oh, I should let BeBe in first."

Outside, I unhooked BeBe from her lead, and she galloped into the house, leaving her snowman behind. Apparently her crush had been fleeting.

I ran up the stairs as she pranced around the living room, licking, slobbering, drooling, and shaking wet fur.

It wasn't long before I heard the front door close and saw the two detectives walking toward the street.

I had the uneasy feeling I'd be seeing a lot more of them.

Eight

In times of stress I take to my drawing pad. And if this wasn't a stressful time, I didn't know what was. Never mind that Kit was missing. Or that Daisy was dead. Or that there was a poultry pestilence going on in the Mill.

No, my brain had already filed away those mind-numbing morsels in a corner labeled Deal with Later.

My current elevated stress hit a little closer to home.

From my spot on the floor, I glanced up at my bed, though I didn't need visual confirmation for what I was hearing.

My mother snored.

So did BeBe.

It was all a girl could do to stay sane.

The forty watt glow of my table lamp was just enough light for me to work. I picked a purple oil pastel out of its case and colored in foxglove. I used my pinkie to blend. I was working on a design board for Alice Graeme, a sweet old lady who'd heard of Taken by Surprise through the Mill's grapevine. She and her sister, May, lived a few blocks over, technically out of the neighborhood, but I'd learned never to underestimate the power of the Mill's gossiping abilities. Alice had hired me to do a backyard make-over for May this coming spring, and my head swam with ideas for the pair.

I stretched out my legs, rolled my shoulders. Under ordinary circumstances my bedroom floor wasn't the ideal place to work. But these weren't ordinary times, and there wasn't anywhere else for me to go.

Downstairs was occupado with Kevin. Downstairs I would feel obligated to talk to him. Downstairs we might have to discuss that phone call I'd overheard.

I was avoiding downstairs like the plague.

Riley's room was off-limits. Never mind the fact that he was in there—Xena was in there. Xena was Riley's pet boa constrictor. We had a love/hate relationship. Mostly, I loved to hate her. The deal was that as long as Riley took care of her, he could live. If, for some reason, Xena managed to escape again, like she did last spring, Riley knew I'd hunt him down.

I had boundaries.

Speaking of boundaries, I rose up on my knees and peered out the bottom of my window at the house across the street. My shade was pulled down three-quarters of the way—just enough to see that the lights were on at Bobby's, as if beckoning me over.

I felt beckoned.

And tempted.

It was odd having Bobby across the street. Don't get me wrong, I loved having him there. But it was strange being *here*, with him *there*. I always felt as though the neighbors knew when I went over—and stayed the night. It was worse than if we'd moved in together.

So, I tried to set limits for myself. Tried to keep things the way they would be if he lived across town and not two hundred feet away.

My mother snorted and rolled over, causing BeBe to snort and roll over too. I thought about taking a picture for this year's Christmas card, but I valued my life.

I sunk back down, trying not to think about Bobby. I shuffled him off into another corner of my brain labeled, Keep Your Pants On. It was a dusty corner, rarely used.

Which said volumes about how well I was doing with the boundaries I'd set with him.

Refocusing on my drawing, I smiled at what I had so far. Since Alice had said May loved whimsy, I was aiming for a fairy garden. Romantic and old-fashioned, with lots of fuss but little muss, because realistically the two women couldn't get around all that well anymore.

I planned a sedum walkway and would fill in empty space with colorful delphiniums, hollyhocks, roses, dianthus, and ferns. I set a section aside for herbs such as rosemary, thyme, and saffron, to scent the air. I hoped my local nursery would have the perfect lichen-covered rock for added atmosphere.

I'd spent the last hour scouring online catalogs for the right accessories. I found a tree-stump shaped as a chair, a weathered whitewashed bench, and a scalloped-shaped fountain complete with a perched fairy, wings spread as she poured water into the bowl, perfect for the garden.

Lighting would be essential to this garden, so I colored in two- and three-stemmed mushroom-shaped lights made from copper I found on an artisan website. I made a mental note to ask Kit to look into—

I stiffened.

Kit.

I tried to shove him back into that corner of my mind he'd snuck out of, but I couldn't. He didn't just loom large in real life, but in my thoughts too.

What was he doing? Was he okay? Scared? Hungry? Grieving all alone?

What had he thought about Kent Ingless? And what exactly had he been doing to help Daisy with her business?

My cell phone vibrated, and I grabbed it and headed into the bathroom.

"Where are you?" Ana asked. "You sound all echoey."

"In the bathroom." I kept my voice low.

"Do I want to know?"

I peeked out my door, at my mother hogging the covers

and BeBe hogging the bed. "No." Closing the door tight, I wondered how I was going to budge BeBe so I could get some sleep. "Where are you?" I asked. Filtered voices came across the line. "What's all that noise in the background?"

"TSA warning about leaving baggage unattended."

I sank into the empty bathtub. "You're coming home?"

"How could I stay away? This is Kit we're talking about. The big galoot."

"Galoot? Have you been drinking?"

"Just a little. Listen, I'm stuck in Denver. There's a blizzard here, and most of the flights into Cincinnati have been canceled because of the snow there. I don't know when I'll be getting in. Can you pick me up?"

I had to smile. Only Ana would ask me to pick her up when she didn't have a clue as to when that might be. "Of course."

And only I would agree without a moment's hesitation.

"How are things there?" she asked.

I filled her in on Kevin, Maddie, Daisy's parents, Lewy and Joe, and the rooster fiasco.

I could hear her pout. "I'm missing everything!"

"Be glad."

"Hmmph. Well, what are you doing tomorrow?"

"Perry and I are going to talk to Kent Ingless. See what he knows."

"Can't you wait until I get in?"

"We'll see."

"I miss everything!"

We said our good-byes, and I climbed out of the bathtub.

I yawned as I gathered up my drawing supplies and set them on my nightstand in the bedroom. Crossing over to the window, I knelt down and looked across the street. Then I glanced back at my bed, where there was no room for me.

It made sense to go over there.

Perfectly justifiable.

It would be so nice to curl up with Bobby. There was something about being in his arms that made me feel safe and secure and . . . loved.

But there were those pesky boundaries.

What was a girl to do?

Making up my mind, I went into the closet and pulled down an extra blanket. I wrestled my pillow out from beneath BeBe's head, hoping she didn't drool in her sleep, and settled in on the floor.

As I turned off the lamp, I told myself my decision had everything to do with maintaining a healthy distance so my and Bobby's relationship could grow.

But I knew as I fell into a fitful sleep it had more to do with not wanting to have to deal with Kevin on my way out.

There were no corners left in my head to store away that information.

I was getting good at sneaking out.

It was all about distraction.

I'd waited until my mother was changing Kevin's gauze, then announced that I'd be taking BeBe for a walk, maybe go check on Gregory Peck, and see if Miss Maisie had contacted the CDC yet.

It was ten in the morning and all was quiet in the Mill. Snow reached mid-calf on my galoshes, but the sun peeped through fluffy clouds, promising a beautiful day. BeBe pranced around the yard, taking a moment to visit her snowman. She'd been having a blast until she saw the turkeys lurking near the woods at the back of my property.

One turkey sighting and she was cowering behind my legs, shaking like a bad Elvis impersonator. Namely, my dad. I wondered if he'd give a performance of "Don't Be Cruel" if my Thanksgiving dinner needed livening up.

As I dragged BeBe toward Mr. Cabrera's, I thought about my father. Was he lonely? I guessed not. I could practically see him lounging in his recliner, watching the History Channel, coffee in one hand, bag of Cheetos in the other.

My mom never let Dad have Cheetos.

I had to know. Pulling out my cell phone, I called him. "Are you eating Cheetos?"

Crunch, crunch. "What? No. Never! Did you know on this day in 1835 the horseshoe manufacturing machine was patented?"

"No. And I'd wipe the cheesy fingerprints off the phone before Mom gets home." To the dog, I said, "C'mon, BeBe!"

She'd planted all four paws in the snow.

"She's not coming home, is she?" Dad didn't have to specify the "she." I could tell by the fear in his voice.

"I don't know," I lied, tugging on BeBe. It wasn't easy budging 150 pounds of turkey-fearing canine.

"What do you mean you don't know? Didn't you see your mother this morning?"

My breath puffed out in front of me like little evil cumulous clouds. "Actually, I didn't."

Lying again. I suppose it was bad enough to lie, but to lie and enjoy it? Maybe I had a sadistic streak.

If I did, it was easily explained by the fact that he'd gone and left my mother with me. I was going to need to see a chiropractor if I had to sleep on the floor again.

His voice tinged in panic, he said, "I've got to go, Nina."

"'Bye, Dad."

I flipped my phone closed, tucked it into my pocket. A light coat of snow had covered BeBe.

"Come on, Beebs." I yanked, I tugged, I begged, I cajoled. Finally, I said, "Gobble, gobble!"

She leaped forward, nearly knocking me down in the process. Barking, she wound her way around me, wrapping me like a mummy.

"BeBe, stop!"

She was having fun now, the little devil.

Just when I was wondering how I was going to get out of that mess, I heard, "Ach. There's a good schnitzel."

Great. Just great.

BeBe lunged for Brickhouse.

"Timber!" she yelled, cackling.

As I fell, I suddenly remembered why I didn't like that woman.

She laughed and laughed. "I wish I had a camera. What a great Christmas picture this would be for my cards this year."

Ugh. I didn't want to think Mrs. Krauss and I were alike at all, but there were times . . .

I shoved those thoughts into the Never Be Thought About Again, Ever corner.

BeBe easily pulled me across the snow, as though I was some bound-up Christmas tree she was delivering.

I looked up at Brickhouse. "You're not going to leave me like this, are you?"

She clucked. "Depends."

"On?"

"Are you sneaking off?"

"Ha. Ha. Who says I snuck off?"

She held up her hand. One chubby finger shot into the air. "The detectives." Another finger. "Your mother." Another finger. "Tam."

Tam! She'd ratted me out?

Another finger. "Kevin."

"All right! All right! I snuck off." My backside was starting to freeze.

She planted meaty hands on her hips. "I want to go with you today."

I wiggled, trying to free myself. It wasn't pretty. "I don't think so."

"Suit yourself, Nina Ceceri."

She turned and started walking away. BeBe followed, dragging me along.

I caved. "All right! You can come."

She clucked happily as she unleashed BeBe and unwound me. "Where are we going?"

I explained about Kent Ingless.

"How are we going to lose the fuzz?" She motioned to the curb. Lewy and Joe sat in a dark Taurus.

Wonderful.

"Fuzz?" I asked. "Really?"

"Are you one to question my word choices?"

She had a point. I followed her to Mr. Cabrera's house, and true to my word, I checked on Gregory Peck. He seemed to be doing well, having taken over the garage for his roost.

"Where's Mr. Cabrera?"

"Ach. Walked himself to the hardware store. He's intent on catching those turkeys."

I smiled. When Mr. Cabrera had his mind set on something, he usually went at it gung ho.

Brickhouse pulled on a rainbow-colored knit cap. "What's our plan of escape?"

It was scary how much enjoyment she was getting out of this. I swore I caught her humming the theme song to *Mission Impossible* while filling a bowl of water for BeBe.

"Leave BeBe here, mosey over to Miss Maisie's to make sure she's okay after the rooster debacle yesterday, then sneak out her back door to meet up with Perry." I checked my watch. "We have ten minutes."

My phone chirped. Bobby.

"Were you and BeBe playing Iditarod?" he asked.

I looked out Mr. Cabrera's front window and could see Bobby standing in his window, phone in one hand, coffee cup in the other. "Very funny. Where's your shirt?"

"Just got out of the shower."

My mouth went dry.

Softly, he said, "I left the lights on for you last night."

Damn those boundaries. "Will they be on again tonight?"

"Probably."

I was glad to hear it. I saw him take a sip of coffee, wince. "You should really blow on that first. Dinner tonight?" I asked.

He laughed. "Sure, I should be home by then. I'm headed down to Mac's place—promised I'd watch the Bengals game with him."

"Okay."

"Dare I ask what you're doing today? I assume it will have something to do with outwitting the two detectives in front of your house."

"Something like that."

"The less I know, the better?"

I smiled. "Definitely."

I hung up, and Brickhouse and I headed toward Miss Maisie's.

She seemed surprised to see us, and even more surprised when we said hello, asked how she was, and wondered aloud if we could leave through her back door.

She showed us out, but not before checking to see if there were any stray fowl running around outside.

We picked our way through the deep snow, cutting through Mrs. Greeble's backyard.

As we neared the back of the house, something caught my eye. I crept up to the window and looked in.

"Nina!" Brickhouse whispered loudly. "What are you doing? Time is of the essence, child."

I stood there, unable to believe what I was seeing.

"What has you so captivated?" She came up behind me. "Ah." She clucked. "Oh."

I couldn't have said it better.

Right there in Mrs. Greeble's back room was a large poker table.

Now I knew why Riley had been spending so much time with her.

Nine

As Brickhouse and I trudged through the snow, all I could think about was Riley. How he'd fooled me once again. And my first evil thought was like father, like son, but as soon as I thought it, I was ashamed. It wasn't fair to lump Kevin's sins on Riley.

I stomped along, feeling petulant. I had believed I'd come a long way in parenting a teen. I'd picked up tricks to spot lies, tips to weasel information.

I'd been blindsided by this, thinking, believing, that Riley was helping Mrs. Greeble. That he was *earning* his money. Not *winning* it.

And don't get me started on Mrs. Greeble. She'd seemed so nice, yet if she was running a poker game out of her house, she had to have a dark side.

Now I felt the obligation to figure out how dark.

Just one more thing for me to worry about.

"You look like your head is about to pop off. It's not attractive, Nina Ceceri." Brickhouse glanced back at me as she held a branch so it wouldn't thwap me in the face. "Perhaps all is not what it seems."

I arched an eyebrow, my BS meter working on overdrive.

"On occasion," she clucked, "I am wrong. It's rare, occurring about as often as a harvest moon, but it does happen. This may well be one of those times."

"You think?"

"No need for snippiness." Releasing the branch, she forged ahead.

Snow seeped down into my galoshes, absorbed into my jeans. Ask me last week, and I'd have said there was little worse than wet jeans. This week I held a whole new perspective on life's pitfalls.

Though the jeans still ranked up there.

"Sorry," I grumbled. "I just don't know what's worse. That he's been gambling for money or that I keep being duped by him."

Her laughter carried back to me. "Teenagers are created to dupe parents."

"Did Claudia ever dupe you?" I asked, referring to her grown daughter.

"Ach. No. I'm too smart to fall for such things."

I tried to step in the prints Brickhouse made. "Gee, thanks."

"I'm sure it's not what we think. Talk to him before you accuse him of anything."

As we emerged from our journey through the Mill's backyards, I decided not to think about it for a while. I'd deal with Riley later.

A small Saturn, circa 1992, sat at the curb, idling. Thick, crispy street salt adhered to the car like dried out barnacles. Chunks of dirty snow clung to the car's wheel wells, and two inches of thick snow covered the hood, roof, and trunk like a wintry blanket.

The passenger window rolled slowly down. Inside, I saw Perry leaning across the front seat, cranking the lever.

Brickhouse and I gaped.

"Where's the Range Rover?" I asked.

"Get in, get in," he ordered. "I've been sitting here for ten minutes and the car won't heat unless it's moving. I've lost feeling in the tip of my nose! Hurry, hurry! I like this nose. I paid a lot of money for this nose."

"Shotgun!" Brickhouse called, yanking open the front door.

I rolled my eyes and pulled open the back door. The handle, also caked in salt, felt starchy and stiff under my fingers. I rubbed my hands down my pants and made a face at my damp, clingy jeans.

I was seriously missing summertime.

Perry air-kissed Brickhouse's cheeks but didn't ask why she was there. He shifted, the gears grinding. Tires spun as he stepped on the gas. The car spurted forward, then stopped, stalled.

"The Range Rover?" I winced as the gears ground.

"You wouldn't believe it," he said. The rosy color of his cheeks stood out against the black hat he wore. It had a large rounded crown and drooping ear flaps, and looked like he'd stolen it from the Red Baron's closet.

The car lurched and I flew forward, almost ending up in the front seat. And I nearly got whiplash when the car died again, sending me backward.

I fastened my seat belt, tightening it around my waist.

Perry cursed a blue streak, banging the steering wheel. He ended his diatribe with a vicious jerk of the gear shift and the threat of, "Don't make me get out and kick your rotten, stinkin', rusty chassis," before Brickhouse reached over and turned off the ignition.

"Get out," she ordered Perry as she opened her door.

I watched in amazement as he obeyed. I'd never even heard him raise his voice before. He slowly walked around the front of the car as Brickhouse crossed behind. He wore a thick cable-knit Irish wool sweater, jeans, and a wool coat that hit him mid-thigh.

Brickhouse sat in the driver's seat while Perry took a minute to stomp the extra snow off his Doc Martens before getting back into the car.

"Seat belts," Brickhouse intoned, using a voice I hadn't heard since tenth grade English.

Perry buckled in a hurry.

"Where to?" she asked, sending a stream of wiper fluid onto the windshield to clear away the film of dried salt.

I thought that maybe, just maybe, I'd never use salt again.

I gave her the directions I'd memorized. It had taken Tam no time at all to track down Kent's address.

Brickhouse started the car, revved the engine, and slowly pulled into the street, where previous brave drivers had left gullies to guide us through the snow.

Perry looked back at me and smiled as though nothing out of the ordinary had taken place. "As I was saying, you wouldn't believe it."

He was probably right. I kind of didn't believe my life lately.

"There I was getting ready to pick you up, but first I had to shovel the driveway. Straight downhill, you know, and if the snow isn't removed immediately, it will ice, and then I'd never be able to get the Range Rover back into the carport."

"The horror," Brickhouse deadpanned.

Perry cupped his mouth. "Is she cranky today?"

I didn't bother to lower my voice. "She's cranky every day."

Brickhouse clucked.

"Go on," I said to Perry.

"There I was shoveling away when I saw it."

"It?" I asked.

Perry fiddled with the heat. "Them, really. Footprints. Can you believe it?"

"Well, maybe?" I said, not sure what he was getting at.

"Leading up to my carport and away again."

"Oh?" Brickhouse said, keeping her hands at ten and two.

"I followed them." Perry cranked up the heater. "I mean, nobody had any business near my car. I mean, hello? Private property."

I smiled. I couldn't help it. "And?"

"They led to the front of my car, which I thought was a bit odd, no?"

"Very odd," I encouraged.

I thought I saw Brickhouse smile, but couldn't be sure. Could have been indigestion. One never knew with her.

Perry went on. "I looked around, but didn't see anything unusual. The car was still locked, everything looked well and good, but I couldn't figure it out. Why walk up to my car and walk away again?"

Beats me.

"So I took a closer look," Perry said, his eyes wide.

I realized he was enjoying telling this story, feeding us bits at a time, leading up to . . . who knew?

"I went over it with a fine-tooth comb, top to horribly dirty bottom. My car needs a wash desperately. Is there anything more disgusting than a salt-encrusted vehicle? Is there?" The flaps on his hat bounced as he looked between the two of us.

"Your story-telling skills," Brickhouse proclaimed, tugging off her hat. Tufts of white hair stuck out in all directions. "Get on with it."

To her, he said, "You're lucky I love you, Ursula."

She clucked. "I was thinking the same thing, Perry."

I bit back a grin as he cupped his mouth again and whispered to me, "Cranky," while gesturing to Brickhouse with his thumb.

I nodded.

Thankfully, he continued. "While examining the undercarriage of the Rover and bemoaning the fact that my car, my baby, needed a bath, something caught my eye." He paused for dramatic effect. "It was . . . a GPS unit."

I let that sink in.

"What's a GPS?" Brickhouse asked.

"I'll tell you what it is," Perry said excitedly. "It's a tracking device. Someone wanted to follow me. Or more appropriately," he held my gaze, "you. Someone who knew we were together yesterday, perchance?"

"The good detectives? You think?"

"Who else?" Brickhouse asked. "You never were the brightest bulb."

"Hey now," I said. "You are cranky."

"I told you so." Perry preened.

He settled back into his seat as I tried not to think who else would want to track me. I felt fairly safe being followed by the police. If the person who'd killed Daisy was on my trail, however, well that'd be enough to send me hitchhiking to Denver to hide out with Ana.

I took a second to ponder all the things I was trying not to think about. The list was adding up. Which was fine with me—as long as I didn't think about it.

"Being the noble man I am," Perry said, "I set aside my own needs for the sake of our investigation and borrowed Mario's car!"

"This is Mario's?" I asked, taking in the cracked seats, the old radio.

Perry sighed. "He has an attachment to it. I tried long ago to get him to trade it in, to no avail. But I make him park it on the street."

"Ach, yes. Very noble of you," Brickhouse murmured.

Kent Ingless lived a few miles from Heavenly Hope. With the roads a mess, it took nearly an hour to get there from my house, usually a fifteen minute drive.

A long recently plowed driveway wound up to the house, a gorgeous log Gambrel. Twin dormer windows peeked out from the second floor, and a bay window on the first floor had its drapes pulled. However, smoke came from the stack-stone chimney, and the walkway was freshly shoveled. "Looks like he's home."

Brickhouse parked. "Do we have a plan?"

Perry looked at me.

"Well, ah, no," I said. "We're just going to play it by ear."

Brickhouse's blue eyes chilled. I hated when they did that. "What makes you think he will let us in?"

Perry rummaged in the trunk. "Well, listen to Miss Optimism."

The icy blue stare turned on him. "We're perfect strangers. Why would he have any reason to speak with us?"

I hated when she made sense.

Producing a tray with a flourish, Perry said, "Because I've got cannoli. Who can turn down cannoli?"

Not me. My mouth watered.

Brickhouse clucked. "I like you, Perry. You come prepared. Unlike other people I know." She glanced my way.

"You could have stayed home," I tossed over my shoulder as I marched up the walkway, my wet jeans chafing my thighs.

I knocked loudly on a wooden door inset with beautiful stained glass. Through it I saw a figure moving closer.

The door inched open.

I wasn't sure what I had been expecting a boyfriend of Daisy's to look like. Okay, I pictured someone like Kit. Big and bulky. Or maybe even the hippie type. Long hair, Birkenstocks, free-thinking mentality . . .

The man who stood in the doorway wore crisp Ralph Lauren pressed pants, a cashmere sweater, and a look that said, "Go away." He appeared to be of Mediterranean descent, with short silver gray hair, an olive skin tone, and dark eyes. He wasn't short, wasn't tall, wasn't fat, wasn't thin. Average, all around.

"Hi," I said brightly, as if I were there selling cookies and not asking about murder. "I know you don't know us, but I'm Nina Quinn, this is Perry, and this is Ursula." I smiled in a friendly we're-not-serial-killers kind of way.

Piercing black eyes focused on me. "Jesus."

He'd said it in a tone that would earn him penance from Father Keesler at St. Valentine's.

"I know who you are," Kent said to me.

Perry held up his offering. "I brought cannoli."

Kent Ingless fisted a hand, released it.

I fidgeted. "We just want to ask you a few questions."

"About Kit?" he asked through clenched teeth.

"I knew you looked to be a man of intelligence," Brickhouse said, brushing past him into the house without an invitation.

Perry followed.

Kent looked at me, something dark and dangerous in his eyes. The hair on the back of my neck stood on end, and I thought maybe grabbing Perry and the cannolis and getting the heck out of Dodge might be the wisest decision.

Brickhouse could fend for herself.

"We could come back another time," I mumbled.

"But you're here now," he said so sweetly that it reminded me of the witch luring Hansel and Gretel into the gingerbread house. "Come in out of the cold."

If he so much as cackled, I was out of there.

"Um, thanks." Inside, welcoming scents of vanilla and sage filled the air. Though dark, because all the drapes had been drawn, the house had a cozy air about it, completely at odds with the doom and gloom vibe I picked up from Kent.

Perry had set his plate on the coffee table, an old steamer trunk, and taken a seat next to Brickhouse on a buttercream-colored couch. I opted to sit in a wingback across from them, and Kent sat in a thickly upholstered rocking club chair that creaked with every motion.

The fireplace offered light. The burning logs crackled and spit, each noise as loud as a freight train in the silence of the room.

Kent made no motion to set out plates or offer drinks, and it didn't take my impeccable Clue playing skills to recognize that we weren't welcome, cannoli or not.

I took a deep breath since no one else seemed to be starting the conversation. "First, our sympathies on Daisy's passing."

Brickhouse clucked.

I was glad Kent didn't know Brickhouse and probably couldn't decipher her clucks as well as I could. That was definitely a cluck of disagreement.

I pressed on. "Kit's a good friend of ours. We're worried about him."

"You don't think he killed Daisy?" An eyebrow arched as the chair creaked. My hair still stood on end. This guy was creepy with a capital C.

"No, we don't," I said.

"I see. And you're here, why?" Kent asked.

My flight or fight instinct leaned toward flight. I fidgeted in my chair. "Honestly? Your and Daisy's relationship was news to us. We were hoping you might be able to—"

"What?" *Creak creak.* "Confess?"

I gulped. "I don't think, I don't mean, that's not what I—"

Brickhouse was a little more straightforward. "Did you do it?"

Creak. Slowly, enunciating each word, he said, "Do I look capable of . . . *murder*?"

Perry picked this time to finally say something. "Holy hell, yes, honey. I mean, you're a mighty fine looking guy, but those eyes. I nearly wet myself sitting over here." He stood. "I'm just going to take my cannoli and wait in the car." Rushing to the door, he mumbled something about nightmares and Christopher Walken.

Brickhouse looked at me as the door slammed. "I don't think he should be left alone. I'll be in the car too." She hustled out of the room faster than I thought a woman of her size and girth could move.

The door slammed again.

I was alone with Kent.

Talk about fending for yourself.

Again he arched the eyebrow, narrowed evil eyes. "Looks like," *creak creak*, "we're all alone."

A log tumbled in the fireplace, sending sparks flying and my nerves over the edge. Perry wasn't alone—I thought maybe I might wet myself too.

I crossed my legs, my jeans protesting, and forced myself not to be scared to death. "How did you meet Daisy?"

"Through work." *Creak creak.*

"What exactly do you do?" Besides scare the hell out of people?

"I'm a chef of sorts."

Of sorts? What did that mean? "I don't suppose you'd care to elaborate?"

"No."

"All right. How long had you two been together, you and Daisy?"

"Six months." His rocking had slowed, each creak extending into more of a scream.

How appropriate.

I thought about the six months. Daisy had still been with Kit for most of that time. "Did you love her?"

Not so much as a blink from him. "Yes."

"Do you know who killed her?"

Creeeeeaaaak. "No."

"Do you know how Kit was helping Daisy? At work?"

"No."

Liar, liar, but he'd pass a lie-detector test easy. "Do you think Kit killed her?" I asked.

"I don't know."

I brought out the question I really wanted answered. "Do you think her death could be tied to the drugs she sold?"

The chair creaked one last time as he rose. "It's time for you to leave."

Not liking him looming over me, I jumped to my feet. "But—" I protested.

"We're done."

"You're hiding something," I accused, hoping he wouldn't notice my knees knocking.

"Daisy never liked you."

I drew in a breath. "She didn't even know me!"

"She thought Kit was too attached to you, too loyal. She was jealous."

"Why are you telling me this?"

He opened the door. "Oddly, I find that I happen to like

you, Ms. Quinn. I like your spunk, the fire in your eyes,
your loyalty to your friend. I like that you want to do right
by him, see justice served. Those are qualities hard to come
by."

I didn't want to know the way he treated the people he
didn't like.

"It's time for you to leave, Nina," he said in a soft, scary
whisper. "I suggest you stay out of this. Daisy was killed
and the same could easily happen to you."

The threat was clear.

I would have run to the car, but my knees were shaking
too hard. Once in, Brickhouse stepped on the gas, sending
the car fishtailing and snow flying.

She straightened out and zoomed down the driveway.
"He's guilty. I can sense these things. I didn't suffer through
two years of Matthew de la Cruz in English Lit not to know
when someone's guilty."

"Did you see that steamer trunk?" Perry asked. "I bet
there was a body in there! Don't people burn sage to ward
off evil?"

Brickhouse shifted into second when she reached the
main road. "There's evil, then there's *evil*. No amount of
sage would work on that man."

I spotted the platter of cannoli, took its wrapper off. "Yet
you left me alone with him."

"You are woman!" Perry said, shaking a fist in the air.

"You are chicken," I countered, biting into the cannoli.

"Self-preservation, sugar."

"You're lucky you brought these cannoli with you."

I needed them. I tossed the information Kent had given
me on top of everything else I was trying so hard not to
think about.

I wondered how long before it all toppled down on me.

"Did you see those eyes?" Brickhouse asked. "Evil, I tell
you." She crossed herself. When she took her hand off the
wheel, the car drifted right. She yanked left to correct, and
the car fishtailed, its tires losing traction. We spun in three

circles, the car slipping, sliding toward a large oak tree off the side of the road. I closed my eyes and wished I hadn't eaten that cannoli.

The crunch of metal and the sound of breaking glass shattered the eerie silence. I lurched forward, then back again as the car jerked to a halt, its front end resting against the oak's trunk. Well, smushed into the trunk would be a better description.

We sat there for a stunned minute. Everyone was okay, that was the most important thing. No injuries, just a little tossed and shaken.

For some reason I thought a martini sounded good right about now.

"Mario's going to kill me," Perry murmured.

Neither Brickhouse nor I disputed that.

Perry looked back at me, his gray-green eyes big and wide. "Maybe I can stay at your house?"

I unbuckled my seat belt. "The inn's full."

"Ach. You can stay with me," Brickhouse said.

I thought I'd rather face Mario's wrath.

A car pulled up alongside of us, a dark Taurus. "Oh no," I murmured.

"How'd they find us?" Brickhouse asked.

I groaned. "Perry, did you happen to check Mario's car for a GPS?"

"Oops."

Ten

I was sandwiched in the middle of the Taurus's backseat between Brickhouse and Perry. A tow truck was called to retrieve Mario's car but hadn't arrived by the time we left the scene, and I think Perry was seriously considering staying with Brickhouse for the night.

I thought he might need medical attention, but he shooed off offers to take him to the E.R.

"You know," Lewy said, "driving in a level three snow emergency is against the law unless it's actually an emergency. I could take you in."

I rolled my eyes.

"And Nina, we warned you about interfering in our investigation."

"I'm not investigating, Lewy. I'm asking questions."

"Well, stop," Joe said.

"I'll stop as soon as you start looking at other suspects. Kit didn't kill Daisy."

Brickhouse clucked.

Since Lewy seemed the saner of the two, I said to him, "What if Eva were accused of killing someone? And then went missing?" Eva was Lewy's wife. A sweet little thing who adored him.

"It's not the same, Nina. Eva isn't cheating on me."

"Kit and Daisy weren't dating anymore." I leaned forward, jabbed a finger in the air. "And don't tell me that's just another motive. I don't want to hear it. There are other people who might want to kill Daisy."

"Like who?" he asked.

"That Kent Ingless is one scary man," Perry piped in.

Joe flipped on a blinker. The scanner was turned down low, barely audible. Below the dash, a computer screen was lit up. I wondered when detecting had gone high-tech. "More reason for you to stop snooping. It's dangerous. Leave it to the professionals."

"Ach. Like you two? Who prefer to follow us around in hopes we lead you to your prime suspect? What kind of detecting is that?"

Perry slinked closer to the door. I can't say I blamed him. Brickhouse was pushing the limits.

I was surprised when Lewy laughed. "So far, not very good."

"Then why do it?" I asked.

"It's my job," he said. There was something in his voice I couldn't put a finger on.

"Then quit," I mumbled.

Joe chuckled and said something that sounded like "Leah."

"What did you say?" I asked. I only knew one Leah. Leah Quinn, Kevin's first wife. She died when Riley was three. Kevin met and married me five years later.

Brickhouse turned toward me. "He said you're a lot like Leah. Who's Leah?"

My stomach curled. For years I'd wanted to know more about Leah Quinn, but had recently decided to stop wondering about the woman Kevin married first. It wasn't healthy, and knowing wouldn't change anything. It had been pure nosiness on my part.

"Kevin's first wife," I answered.

"What happened to her?" Perry asked.

"She died," Joe answered. "A long time ago."

"How?" Brickhouse asked.

"A boating accident on the river." My nosiness got the better of me. "You knew her well?" I asked Lewy.

"Fairly. Through Kevin. She was a great cop."

"Cop?" I asked.

Lewy shifted in his seat. "You didn't know?"

I shook my head. I'd never even seen a picture of her. "How am I like her? Do I look like her?"

"God, no," Joe said. "She was a stunner."

Great boost to my ego.

"Actually, she looks a lot like G-lo," he added.

"G-lo?" Perry asked.

"Ginger Barlow. Kev's new—"

Perry cut Joe off. "I know who she is."

Joe tapped his fingers on the wheel as if in rhythm to a song only he could hear. "Could be sisters, those two."

Lewy nodded. "Now that you say so, I can see it."

My teeth hurt from clenching them. "So how is it we're alike?"

"Personality," Joe said as if that was low on his list of qualities in women. "A go-getter, that Leah was."

"Feisty," Lewy supplied.

I wondered if feisty was a good thing.

"Nosy," Joe said.

Ah. Now I saw where this conversation was headed.

"It made her a good cop," Lewy added. "The thing is, Nina, you're not a cop. Your nosiness can get you hurt. I don't want to be the one bringing that news to Kevin. I think he's been through enough lately without having to deal with all that."

The old guilt trick.

My mother would have been proud of these two, but it made me feel sick. I didn't belong to Kevin.

I wondered if they'd rehearsed this little tête-à-tête just so I would fall into line and stay out of the investigation.

And I wouldn't doubt for a minute that Kevin put them up to it.

"And Riley," Joe said loudly. "That boy thinks of you as a mom now. Gotta be thinking about him too."

I willed myself not to be swayed by the guilt, though I had to admit using Riley was a good tactic.

Only this wasn't about me. Or Kevin. Or Riley. It was about Kit.

I kept my mouth shut. There was no use arguing my case. Unless I could prove otherwise, Kit was going to jail for murder.

The thought depressed me. I slumped back in my seat.

In a rare burst of sympathy, Brickhouse murmured, "Ach, it'll be okay."

Perry patted my hand, then turned his full attention to the detectives, his woes over Mario's car apparently left with the wreckage. "I want to hear more about Leah," he said, practically bouncing in his seat.

Lewy and Joe seemed to latch on to this idea. Great.

During the agonizing ride home, I had to endure how-she-saved-the-day stories, how-she-and-Kevin-fell-in-love-at-the-police-academy stories, her-being-pregnant stories (God, just kill me now and be done with it), and finally, after all these years, I heard the whole story of how she died.

I cursed Mother Nature and the snow and all things that made this ride take so long.

My stomach tossed and turned, and I was seriously regretting the cannoli. This was what I'd wanted, to hear details, to know the woman who was so much a part of Riley . . . and Kevin. But now?

I felt sick. I didn't want to listen. It was easier dealing with the ghost of a woman I barely knew. It was another thing thinking about her as someone I probably would have been friends with.

I wanted to block my ears and sing "Lalalalala" at the top of my lungs until Lewy finished the story of how Kevin, Riley, and Leah had been celebrating Riverfest on a friend's boat, watching the fireworks, when another boat collided with theirs, flipping it.

Of how it had taken Kevin a few minutes to find Riley in the murky Ohio River.

Of how Leah never surfaced.

Of how they looked for her body for weeks, never finding it.

Of how Kevin nearly went mad with grief.

And of how, as his friends, Lewy and Joe never wanted to see that happen to him again.

By the time the pair dropped us off at my house, I practically crawled over Perry to get out of the car.

As much as I hated to admit it, the guilt was working.

And when I walked into the house, saw Kevin sitting on the couch looking pale and drawn, bags under his eyes, with Riley next to him, with a goofy grin on his face from something his dad had said, I forgot all about the things I was mad about and forced myself not to rush over and pull them both into hugs. Instead, I did the next best thing.

I burst into tears.

My mother rushed in from the kitchen, took one look at me and gathered me in her arms, pushing my head into her ample bosom.

Sometimes there was nothing like a mother's hug, and thinking so just made me cry all that much harder on Riley's behalf.

Finally, I pulled away and accepted a handkerchief from Perry, who had followed me inside.

My mother jabbed a finger in Kevin's direction. "What did you do?"

"Me?" Shock lifted his eyebrows. "Nothing!"

My mother cursed in French. I didn't have to know the language to understand what she was saying.

"It's true," Riley said, jumping to his feet. "She just came in and started with the tears." He looked horrified, and took a step away from me as though my emotional outburst might be contagious.

"Ach, it wasn't them. Not directly, at least," Brickhouse said, closing the door behind her.

I hoped Lewy and Joe had gone away. Far, far away.

"Directly? What does that mean?" Kevin demanded.

Perry perched on an armchair. "It was those detectives talking about— Ow!" He glared at Brickhouse. "Why'd you do that?"

"What?" she asked innocently.

"Kick my shin! I bruise easily, you know."

"Oh, I must have slipped. Snow on my shoes," she mumbled.

My mother crossed her arms and aimed her evil eye at the whole group. "What's going on?"

Perry looked at Brickhouse. Both said, "Nothing."

"What was that comment about the detectives?" Kevin asked. By the look in his eye, he wasn't giving up until he got some answers.

I didn't want to stick around for that conversation. There's only so much I could take in a day. Honest. It had nothing to do with Kevin finding out I'd snuck off again, taking Larry and Moe with me. "I'm going to take a bath."

My mother looked at me, concern drawing down the corners of her eyes.

"I'm okay," I said. "I'm just worried about Kit."

"Yeah, Kit," Perry said, nodding.

Brickhouse clucked.

Suspicion crept into my mother's eyes. I took the stairs two at a time, getting away before being subjected to the Grand Inquisition.

At the top, I paused on the landing and listened, wincing as the questions began. Brickhouse had tremendous fortitude, but it wouldn't be long before Perry caved.

Rubbing my gritty eyes, I headed for my room until I saw Riley's door open wide.

I cocked an ear toward the stairs. Brickhouse was explaining about walking BeBe, visiting Miss Maisie.

I didn't have long.

Creeping into Riley's room, I took a cursory glance around. It was a disaster area. Clothes everywhere, bed a mess, school papers tossed on his desk. I picked one up. It was from September. He rarely threw anything away without a lecture from me first, and I could only stomach those twice a year or so.

The drawers of his desk were stuffed with knickknacks from when he was little, from trips to Kings Island, from old stocking stuffers. I didn't find anything suspicious.

I checked under his mattress and found an old Victoria's Secret catalog underneath. Rolling my eyes, I shoved it back in.

Under the bed, stray socks, old binders, and boxes to his video games lived a happy, content life. I shook some of the boxes, but they were empty.

I didn't have time to check his closet, and I wasn't going near Xena's cage.

Letting out a puff of frustration, I put my hands on my hips. My instincts told me he was up to something. I had to trust them—they were all I had left in my maternal cache.

I'd have to wait until Riley went out again before I could search more thoroughly.

Tiptoeing out of his room, I paused, listening. Perry was talking about how evil Kent had looked.

I hustled into my room, locked the door.

A peek out my front windows showed no signs of Lewy and Joe. A glance out the window next to my bed showed Mr. Cabrera in his backyard chasing the turkeys with what looked to be an oversized butterfly net. BeBe, I noticed, was cowering in Mr. Cabrera's gazebo.

I found myself rooting for the turkeys.

My cell phone rang, and I pried it from my pocket and headed into the bathroom, closing and locking that door as well. One couldn't be too careful.

I turned on the tub and answered, recognizing Ana's number.

"Where are you?" she asked. "Niagara Falls?"

"Bathroom. Taking a bath."

"What's with you and bathrooms lately? Every time I call you're in one."

"Safe haven."

"Ah, right. Kevin."

"And my mom. Don't forget about my mom."

Ana laughed. "I wish I could."

My mother and Ana had a long-standing feud. It wasn't so much a feud as genetics. Ana is the daughter of my father's sister, Rosetta, aka Aunt Rosa. Who my mother happens to detest.

Ana and my mother's relationship was the trickle down effect at its best.

I peeled off my starchy jeans and tossed them onto the floor. With a finger, I tested the bathwater, then turned the faucet toward the H.

"Where are you?" I managed to get my shirt over my head before she answered.

"Still in Denver. I don't think this snow is ever going to stop. At this rate, I don't know if I'll be back before Thanksgiving. I had to wait an hour in line just to charge my cell phone for ten minutes. So talk fast."

"You'll get home," I said, hating the note of sadness in her usually peppy voice.

Static crackled the connection. "How am I supposed to help Kit when I'm stuck here?"

"I'm here," I said, "and I don't know how to help Kit."

I sank into the hot water. Heaven. I pulled the shower curtain to trap the steam. I could hear the sound of the airport's PA system in the background but couldn't make out specific words as Ana asked, "There's been no news?"

Letting the hot water soothe away my stress, I filled her in about Kent Ingless and everything else that had been going on since the last time I spoke with her. Not wanting to rehash the particulars, I left out the part about Leah Quinn.

"What do you think he meant about Daisy trying to do the right thing?" she asked.

"I'm not sure. My best guess is that it has to do with the drugs."

"Not selling them anymore?"

"Could be."

"Could . . . mot . . . "

"You're breaking up, Ana."

"Bet . . . go."

The line went dead.

I flipped my phone closed, set it aside, and turned off the tap.

In the sudden silence, I could hear raised voices from downstairs. Something about investigating and danger.

I tuned it out. Brickhouse could handle herself and protect Perry at the same time.

I wasn't worried.

About them.

I didn't want to think about what was in store for me when I emerged from the tub.

Which got me thinking about all the things I wasn't supposed to be thinking about.

The turkeys.

Gregory Peck.

Brickhouse and I being similar.

Kevin getting married.

Riley possibly gambling.

Daisy having hated me.

Leah Quinn.

Daisy dead.

Kit missing.

Bobby.

Thanksgiving dinner.

I drew in a deep breath, held it, and sank under the water.

I had plans to stay under as long as possible, but a loud noise had me resurfacing. It took a second to realize my mother was at the bathroom door, knocking.

"*Chérie*, can I come in?"

"No!"

Next thing I knew, I heard the door open, then close again. I peeked around the shower curtain, saw my mother perched on the countertop.

"How'd you get in?" I asked, letting the curtain fall back into place.

Her voice echoed. "I have my ways."

Ugh. I wanted to sink back down into the water. "Is everyone still here?"

"Ursula and Perry have gone. Riley went off to help Mrs. Greeble, and Kevin is on the telephone and asked for privacy."

My mind sorted all that out. My first thought was to search Riley's room thoroughly while he was out, but my second was to catch him in the act.

Both options required me getting out of the tub, which I didn't want to do just yet.

"After the tears and all, I thought you may have wanted company."

"Yes, I could see how breaking through two locked doors would give you that impression."

"Snarkiness, my dear, is not becoming. Especially when I have news."

I drew back the curtain, stuck my head out. "News?"

"Maddie Pipe phoned. Daisy's viewing will be held tomorrow. Maddie hoped you would attend. I told her you would."

Leave it to my mother to agree without asking me. I should probably have put up a fuss about it, but I wanted to go, to see who might show up. There was one person I wanted to see in particular, someone who could shed some light on Daisy's business and drug selling.

I hoped she had some of the answers I was looking for.

Eleven

As soon as my mother left, I let the water drain out of the tub, watching it swirl in a little vortex down the drain. I quickly got dressed, blow-dried my hair, and pulled it back into a ponytail. With any luck, I would not be seeing Perry again today. As my hairdresser, he wouldn't be fond of my lack of style.

I'd half expected Kevin to be waiting for me to emerge from the tub, but I could hear him talking with my mother downstairs when I opened my bedroom door.

Sprinting across the hallway, I ducked into Riley's room. I started with his bookshelves. He wasn't much of a reader, so it only took five minutes to flip through all his books. None were hollowed out, and none held anything other than old bookmarks. I did notice one of his books from the local library was overdue by fourteen months. I made a mental note to return it and make Riley pay the late fees from legally earned funds.

I peeked in at Xena, who lay coiled in the bottom of her cage. There wasn't anywhere inside the cage Riley could hide anything of significance, like a wad of cash, so I skipped searching in snake territory.

Okay, who was I kidding? If there'd been a big money-sized mound, I wouldn't have stuck my hand in that tank.

No way, no how.

I checked behind and in his Cincinnati Reds ceramic bank, took a piece off one of his 3-D puzzles and peeped inside, and shuffled around his CDs. Nothing.

Turning my attention toward the closet, I wondered if he'd have taken his stash with him to Mrs. Greeble's house. It made sense that he'd need playing money.

But since I'd gotten started, I found I couldn't stop myself from snooping. Ry's closet was oddly tidy. Shirts hung up, pants folded on a shelf. He had a set of built-in dresser drawers that revealed he might have a bit of obsessive-compulsive disorder in him. Folded tees, neat rows of socks, and sweats were stored, color-coded.

Yet, no money.

At the bottom of the closet, I shook old gym shoes, hoping something would fall out. Still nothing. In the way back, I found a couple of shoe boxes. One was filled with old Pokémon cards that looked like they hadn't seen the light of day in five years. Another box held Hot Wheels, which made me smile. I tugged on the small Nike box at the bottom and checked the label. Size 11, youth. Now he wore size 12, mens.

Noticing writing on the lid, I aimed the box toward a beam of sunlight.

MOMMY was written in childlike block letters.

"Find what you were looking for?" a deep male voice asked from behind me.

"Eee!" I screamed, nearly falling backward out of the closet. I caught my balance, guiltily shoved the shoe box back in, and looked up.

Kevin loomed over me, scowling.

He was a great scowler. It was his eyebrows. When he was mad, they snapped together in a furry vee that nearly dipped down to his nose. Very intimidating. Though once, when I was on pain medication, I thought he looked remarkably like Bert from *Sesame Street*.

I missed that pain medication.

That was damn good stuff.

"Me? Looking? Haha." I jumped to my feet. "I was just, er, cleaning up."

His eyebrows separated, one rising upward.

"Riley's kind of messy, if you hadn't noticed. It's, ah, uh, a fire hazard! Can't be having that." I kicked a shoe into the closet, slammed the door closed, and leaned against it. My pulse pounded in my ears as I produced a fake smile.

His other eyebrow arched.

This wasn't the time to rest on my laurels, whatever laurels were. I needed to go on the offensive and change the subject. Quickly. "Did Ginger get a flight out yet?"

"Oh no you don't, Nina."

My pulse pounded in my throat, reverberated in my ears. "Don't what?"

"You're not changing the subject so easily."

Easy? He thought this was easy? Ha! I edged toward the hallway. "What subject is that?"

"What are you doing in here?"

I took another long step, keeping my back to the wall. "Cleaning."

In one stride he cut off my retreat.

"Does Ginger have any idea when planes will be taking off again? Any chance she's going to forego the trip?" *And come back and take you away?*

He leaned in, nudged up my chin. I noticed he needed to shave, but I wasn't about to volunteer to help him.

"Let's make a deal," he said.

"A deal?"

"How about I tell you what I learned about the crime scene at Heavenly Hope, and you tell me what you're doing snooping in my son's room."

I took offense at the way he'd said "my son," as though I had no claim to Riley at all. Especially since it was Kevin's choice to move out without taking Riley with him—mostly because Riley had wanted to stay with me. However, curiosity won out over my sudden spurt of anger. "Is there news? About Kit?"

"Deal?" he asked.

"All right. Deal."

"You first," he said.

I ducked under his arm so I wouldn't feel so trapped. "Oh no. Uh-uh. I can see the way that would play out."

His deep green eyes glowed. "What? You don't trust me, Nina?"

"Do you really want me to answer that?"

With a smirk he said, "It's okay. I don't trust you either."

"Me! What? I'm the most trustworthy person arou—"

He burst out laughing, and it must have hurt because he doubled over clutching his shoulder, cursing a blue streak.

I crossed my arms as he slumped onto Riley's bed. "Serves you right."

His face regaining color, he said, "For what?"

"For laughing at me."

Shaking his head, he muttered something under his breath I couldn't hear. "I'm not going to win this, am I?"

"Nope."

"Fine. Using a metal detector, the crime scene unit found some spent shells near the tree line of Heavenly Hope's property. They found blood on some of the trees leading into the woods. The blood didn't match Daisy's type."

I sat next to him on the bed, absorbing what he was telling me. Someone else had been shot. Most likely Kit.

"No body, though?"

"No. They did find Kit's car keys in the woods."

"Does Lewy still think Kit's involved in Daisy's death? If he was wounded, doesn't that prove otherwise?"

Kevin started to shrug then must have thought better of it. "I don't know. There's no way of knowing just yet if it's Kit's blood. It could be weeks before we hear."

"Who else's would it be?"

"I don't know, Nina. Try not to worry about it until we get some definitive answers."

Right. Not worry. That'd be the day.

"Your turn," he said.

I couldn't believe I'd agreed to this deal. I didn't want Kevin to know my suspicions about Riley just yet. It was easy to see him barreling across the street, barging into Mrs. Greeble's house and demanding answers. The man had no finesse about him.

Brickhouse had been right—there was no need to accuse Riley just yet. Not until I had a little proof. Proof I'd yet to find. Riley and I had a fragile relationship. I didn't want to destroy it by accusing him of something he didn't do. Innocent until proven guilty and all that.

Of course, I highly suspected guilty.

Kevin elbowed me. "I'm waiting."

Damn. Maybe I could color it in a not-so-bad light. "Well, see, it's about Riley. And Mrs. Gree—"

Riley walked into his room.

Saved! Thank heavens.

He took a look at the pair of us on his bed and said, "Something you two want to tell me?"

I jumped up, but Kevin stayed put. "Nope," I said, "not a thing."

Ry looked to his dad.

"I've got nothing," Kevin said, standing.

"You think you two could take your nothingness somewhere else?"

Since I was eager to leave, I didn't put up a fuss about his rudeness. I took advantage of the fact that Kevin moved at the pace of a slug due to his injuries and hightailed it downstairs.

My mother was on the couch watching *Terms of Endearment* on cable. I grabbed my purse and coat, and slipped on my boots.

"Sneaking out again?" my mother asked.

"If I were, I'd be doing a lousy job of it."

"Snarky, *chérie*."

I rolled my eyes. "I'm going to Kroger." I had four days until Thanksgiving.

Without taking her eyes off Shirley MacLaine, she said, "Could you pick me up some kiwis? I'm having a craving."

As I pulled open the door, I heard Kevin on the stairs. At this point I would have offered to fly to New Zealand to pick them myself just to get out of the house. "Sure thing. I'll be gone awhile."

"Au revoir."

I shut the door behind me, pretending not to hear Kevin calling my name.

The sun had come out and temperatures warmed, slowly melting the snow, leaving a slushy mess on the roads. The Snow Emergency level had dropped to a two, and I definitely considered groceries a pressing need to be on the road.

As did everyone else in the county. All of whom seemed to be heading to the same place as me.

The packed store had been picked clean. I managed to scrounge a few kiwis from the organic produce section. I picked up some apples and oranges too.

As I wended my way down the aisles, I kicked myself for not having made a list before I came. Not that it would have mattered. There was no bread, fresh or frozen. No milk. No cereal except for cream of wheat (which I left on the shelf—I wasn't that desperate). The meat selection had been cleared out. There wasn't a frozen turkey to be seen.

An overhead announcement apologized for the lack of stock, blaming it on the weather and the inability of the store's trucks to travel.

My inner panic alarm sounded. I had close to twenty people coming for dinner on Thursday, and only had kiwis, apples, oranges, Beefaroni, Dr Pepper, and tomato soup to feed them. This didn't bode well for a good first meeting with Bobby's family.

I grabbed what I could, including dog food for BeBe,

managed to spend over a hundred dollars despite the fact I barely had anything in the cart, and headed for my truck.

The craziness inside the store had done the impossible—distracted me from what was going on in my life. Namely, the news that Kit had probably been shot. I held on to the hope that no body had been found. Before I gave myself an ulcer, I decided I was going to ask Maddie Pipe, point-blank, if she'd been in contact with Kit. If she had, maybe I wouldn't need to use the bottle of Pepto I just bought.

I piled grocery bags into the cab of my truck and thought back to that box in Riley's closet.

If Kevin hadn't caught me snooping, would I have opened it?

I'd like to think I wouldn't. That I wouldn't invade Riley's privacy in such a manner.

Yet I also knew myself better. I definitely would have looked.

It didn't mean I was happy about it.

As I drove toward home I noticed a familiar car in my rearview mirror. I wasn't quite sure why Joe and Lewy continued to follow me around. It made no sense. They had to know by now I didn't know where Kit was. I wasn't that good a liar.

I pulled into my driveway, Joe and Lewy pulling in behind me.

My gaze automatically went to the house across the street, and I noticed Bobby was home. My heartbeat kicked up a notch.

Riley came out of the house, didn't say hello, grabbed several bags and headed back into the house as Lewy stepped out of the Taurus and came up to me. Joe stayed in the car, talking on his cell phone.

"Is it really necessary to keep following me around?" I asked Lewy.

"Just following orders, Nina."

I pressed a forty pound bag of dog kibble into his arms. "Bring that in, will you?"

Grabbing two bags of groceries, I headed toward the house.

Lewy heaved the bag over his shoulder. "I don't think this is in my job description."

"Might as well make yourself useful. Careful on the steps, they're slick."

"We found your truck," he said as I stepped onto the porch.

I played up my acting skills. "Did you find Kit with it?"

"No. The truck was abandoned on a Georgia freeway, out of gas. Does Kit have family in that area?"

"Not that I know of." I hoped the media attention would latch onto this. It was wrong of me, I know, but anything I could do to help Kit out was worth it.

"When are you leaving?" I asked.

"Leaving?"

"To go look for Kit?"

"We sent a team down."

Damn! Talk about a backfire. "I see."

"And you haven't heard from him?" Lewy asked.

"Wouldn't you know if I had?"

"You're a sneaky one," he said, smiling.

I stepped into the house, passing Riley as he went out for the last of the groceries.

Kevin sat on the couch, bundled up in an afghan. I gave him only the briefest look, trying not to make eye contact. Eye contact was dangerous.

My mother stood in the kitchen, sorting the goods, tsking at the selection of Chef Boyardee I'd made. "Trust me," I said to her. "It was the best I could do."

I heard Kevin and Lewy exchange hellos before Lewy stepped into the kitchen and set down the dog food.

My mother ooohed over her kiwi.

"Don't ask," I told Lewy when he saw her making such a fuss.

Riley placed the last of the groceries on the counter and hopped over the back of the sofa, landing next to Kevin.

"What have you got there?" Lewy asked, coming up behind them.

Curious, I followed. I took a look and wished I'd stayed in the kitchen.

Riley's "Mommy" box sat on the coffee table, its contents strewn across Kevin's and Riley's laps.

"Just a trip down memory lane," Kevin said, glancing at me.

I felt a wee bit sick.

My mother's hand settled on my shoulder. "It's been a long time coming, no?" she said to Riley, fluffing his hair.

He smoothed it down. "I guess."

His surly tone held no true anger. Just one look into his shining eyes and it was easy to see how he'd longed for years to know more about his mother.

I could have kicked myself for not seeing it sooner.

And kicked Kevin for keeping Leah's memory locked away so long.

But that didn't mean I wanted to stick around and hear more gooey, goopy, sappy stories. I had a weak stomach.

I tugged my mother into the kitchen. "I've been thinking—" I began.

"Go, *chérie*. It's where you belong."

I tipped my head. "You didn't even know what I was going to say."

"You were going to say you would stay the night with Bobby. Go, *chérie*. I have things under control here." She kissed my forehead. "Trips down memory lane are good to heal their hearts," she said, nodding to the couch. "However, this is not where your heart belongs. Not right now, at least. Trust Mama."

Like a big sap, I felt my eyes well. "I don't know how you do that," I said.

She shrugged delicately, brushing off my awe. "It's a gift."

I smiled. "It really is."

I ran upstairs, packed a bag. Joe had made his way inside

by the time I made my way downstairs. He, Riley, Lewy, my mother, and Kevin had gathered around the coffee table. A fire blazed from the fireplace, and the whole scene looked awfully cozy.

But it was the last place I wanted to be.

From the back hall, I grabbed a Ziploc bag of doggy kibble, and was headed out the door to collect BeBe before moseying across the street when Kevin's voice stopped me in my tracks.

"Don't forget about our deal," he said from the kitchen doorway. "I can wait until tomorrow."

I smiled weakly and closed the door behind me.

If I had any say in it, he'd be waiting much longer than that.

Twelve

"Holy hell!" I cried, borrowing Perry's phrase, as I opened the door to Bobby's house. The blast of heat nearly knocked me down his front steps.

BeBe pranced and drooled as Bobby came out of the kitchen.

I think I drooled too. He wore nothing but a pair of boxers.

He looked . . . hot. No maybes about it.

And it had nothing to do with the temperature.

Bobby rubbed BeBe's head, murmuring to her about being a good schnitzel.

I wasn't the only one spending too much time with Brickhouse.

Once I pried my gaze from Bobby's sculpted stomach, and the line of hair that trickled from his belly button down beneath the waistband of his Calvin Klein boxers, I found him staring at me.

"Coming in?" he asked.

My mouth had gone completely dry, while my insides felt like they'd dissolved into one of the puddles of melted snow outside.

Absently, I nodded, and closed the door behind me. Placing my bag down, I kicked off my boots, leaving them on a small throw rug, and zipped off my down vest.

Sweat beaded on my forehead. "Why's it so hot in here?"

"Furnace is broken."

I noticed the wrench in his hand then. Funny how I hadn't seen it before.

"Is that dinner?" he asked, gesturing to the Baggie in my hand.

I nodded, unable to keep my gaze from his chest, his abs, and the slight sheen covering both.

He laughed.

"What? Oh." My head snapped up. I smiled. "No," I said, shaking the doggy kibble, "this isn't dinner. Not ours, at least."

BeBe's tail thumped wildly, knocking a lamp off a side table. Luckily, it fell onto the sofa and didn't break.

"I should probably feed her."

She spun in circles.

Bobby laughed again. "Toss it to me."

I did, and BeBe lunged for it, catching it in midair. Doggy kibble flew out everywhere. She crunched and gobbled, sucking every piece she could find from the rug, a canine vacuum.

"I guess that takes care of BeBe." Bobby picked up little plastic bits. "Are you hungry?"

My shirt stuck to me, and my jeans were starting to dampen as well. Twice in one day. Unfair. "I could eat. But I really want to change into something a little cooler."

His blond hair had curled with the humidity in the room, and he looked more tantalizing than ever. Then he winked. "Are you flirting with me, Nina Quinn?"

Oh. My. His wink did something to me. Always had. There was something so seductive in the way he did it. "Maybe." At this rate we wouldn't be eating, and we wouldn't be talking. "Did you fix the furnace?"

"I beat it into submission. It's just going to take a while for the place to cool down."

"Why not open some windows?"

"I thought about it, but then again how often do we get a heat wave in November? Might as well enjoy it. I can make you a margarita."

"Are you flirting with *me*, Bobby MacKenna?"

"Definitely."

Whoo-ee. The temperature in the living room had jumped up another degree or two.

BeBe sniffed out the last of the kibble, and plopped herself on a thick woven rug in front of the brick fireplace. She set her head on her paws, looked up at us, then closed her eyes.

"I'm going to change." I grabbed my bag and headed down the hall to Bobby's room.

"I'll throw a pizza in the oven. How'd today go?"

With a flip of the light switch, Bobby's room filled with a soft glow. We had painstakingly stripped the fifties era wallpaper from the wall, and he'd picked a silvery blue to paint the room. A queen-sized bed with a black mission-style head- and footboard took up most of the small space. Nightstands stacked with books, mostly biographies, flanked both sides of the bed, and a flat screen TV hung from the wall.

Raising my voice, I said, "*Reader's Digest* version or *War and Peace*?"

Pots clanged. *"Reader's Digest."*

"Kent Ingless might be Hannibal Lector in disguise, Riley's probably gambling, if Mario calls you know nothing, Gregory Peck is roosting, and Kevin's first wife is due to be canonized any minute now."

I dropped my bag on the mattress. A plain white down comforter covered half of the unmade bed. White on white checkerboard sheets had been pushed to one side, and I could tell by the disarray he hadn't slept well last night. I wondered if (okay, kinda-sorta hoped) it had been because I wasn't there.

Bobby's shadow fell across the bed, and I turned to find him standing in the doorway, cookie sheet in hand. "Too late for *War and Peace*?"

"How long do you have?"

"For you? All night."

Whoo. Eee. "Then you better get that pizza on."

He grinned and backed out of the doorway.

As I unpacked I filled him in on the day's events. While I told him about Kent, I pulled a sexy nightie from my bag. Putting it on now would be like a neon invitation, one I wanted to save for later.

Biting my thumbnail, I knew I couldn't stay in the clothes I had on. No way. Damp jeans were cruel and unusual punishment.

I pulled off my shirt, choosing to keep my camisole on, and stepped into Bobby's closet, projecting my voice, hoping he could still hear me.

"Kent seems like pure evil, but I can't see a motive for him killing Daisy."

Bobby's voice was muffled. "Unless she knew something he didn't want her to know."

"Like what?" I asked. "The drugs?"

"Probably."

Bobby had installed an organizing system in his tiny walk-in closet that included two built-in dressers, several shelves, two high hanging and two dropped rods.

I opened the top drawer of the closest dresser and pulled a pair of boxers from the crumpled pile. Struggling out of my jeans, I made a mental note to invest in some lounging pants. Maybe sweatpants. Something roomy and comfortable that wouldn't be quite so uncomfortable if wet.

I thought about Daisy and her stand on pharmaceutical therapy. "But she seemed to be okay with the whole drug thing."

"What if what Kent was into wasn't medicinal?"

"Like those little white pills?" I slipped into the cotton boxers and rolled the waistband so they wouldn't fall down. Talk about a neon invitation.

"What?"

Stepping out of the closet, I repeated myself.

Bobby was in the kitchen, filling a bowl with water as I came out. He set it on the floor for BeBe and took a good long look at me.

"Hope you don't mind." I motioned to my CK shorts.

"Mind? Definitely not. You look better in them than I do."

I found that hard to believe. But who was I to argue?

"What pills?" he asked, leaning against the kitchen sink.

I told him about the pills I'd seen near Daisy's body.

Sitting on the kitchen table, swinging my legs, I said, "I'm hoping Ian can help identify what they were. I'm going to see him tomorrow."

Spicy pepperoni smells filled the kitchen as I told Bobby about Leah, who I mostly glossed over, and then revealed my suspicions about Riley.

"You've been doing a lot of work around the neighborhood. Have you noticed anything unusual about Mrs. Greeble?" My legs swung back and forth.

He shook his head. Damp blond curls stuck out in every direction. "She gets a lot of foot traffic, but I chalked it up to people wanting to look out for her. It's pretty amazing that she's eighty-five and still living on her own."

"If it's true she's running an illegal poker room in her house, then she probably doesn't need any financial help. Is there anyone you've seen going in on a regular basis?"

Loud snores came from the living room as BeBe fell into a deep sleep. I smiled and happened to notice a trickle of sweat working its way down Bobby's chest. I'm observant that way.

"Gus brings her lunch every day."

How did I not know this? Gus owned, surprise, surprise, Gus's Diner, a cornerstone in the Mill. "How long does he stay?"

"Don't know. And don't look at me that way," he said with a smile.

"What way?"

He walked toward me. That sweat droplet coasted toward his belly button. Bracing his arms on the table, one on each side of me, he leaned in. "Like you're disappointed. You're the one with the stellar Clue-playing abilities."

Our lips were almost touching. "You're still peeved about losing to me, aren't you?"

"Possibly."

"Will you do me a favor?" I asked.

Our noses touched. "You want me to get into a poker game at Mrs. Greeble's house, don't you?"

I blinked in innocence. "Am I so transparent?"

"Sometimes."

"How about now? What am I thinking?"

"Exactly what I am."

I leaned in just a bit to meet his lips, closed my eyes, and nearly jumped clear out of my skin as the doorbell rang. BeBe's barks echoed through the kitchen, reverberating off the stainless steel fridge.

Bobby hung his head. "So close."

Suddenly I felt as though I were sixteen as I wiggled out from under his arm, afraid my mother was at the door, about to catch me making out with my boyfriend. I shushed BeBe, looked out the front window, and pulled the door open.

"Holy hell!" Perry cried as he stepped inside, trying to push BeBe off him. "It's hot as Hades in here." BeBe licked and slobbered, but finally settled down.

Bobby came in from the kitchen, pulling on a gray T-shirt. The pity.

"Holy hell!" Perry muttered, staring. His gaze flew to mine. "You're one lucky girl."

I arched an eyebrow. "I would have been if you didn't show up."

Perry barked out a laugh that sounded so much like Be-Be's, she jumped up and pranced around. It took a good minute to calm her back down.

"What're you doing here?" I asked him as he kicked off his shoes.

"I can't stay there."

"Where?" Bobby asked.

"With Ursula and Donatelli."

I wasn't the least bit surprised.

Bobby sat on the arm of his couch, a big brown leather number that screamed MANLY MAN. "Why are you staying with them?"

I sat on the coffee table. "That's the whole 'if Mario calls you know nothing' part of my day I haven't had a chance to tell you about."

"Oh." Bobby looked amused, a smile playing at the corners of his mouth.

"The noise," Perry said. "Something's living in their garage—"

"Gregory Peck."

"I'm sorry, sugar, but if Gregory Peck was in there, I'd have been one happy man."

"Gregory Peck is a chicken," Bobby said in a don't-ask kind of voice.

"Actually," I said, "he's a rooster."

"Then the cocka-doodle-dooing makes sense." Perry sank into a taupe armchair. "But the noise coming from Ursula's and Donatelli's bedroom is worse." He shuddered.

I shuddered.

Bobby shuddered.

Perry hung his coat on the doorknob. "Can I stay here?"

Bobby and I looked at each other, and I immediately mourned the noise that wouldn't be coming from Bobby's room that night. "Sure," I said.

Bobby hung his head again.

Perry sniffed the air. "Is something burning?"

Jumping up, Bobby raced into the kitchen just as the smoke alarms wailed.

"Pizza," I said with a grimace.

"Not much of a cook, is he?" Perry whispered.

"He has other talents."

"I'll bet."

I heard a kitchen towel flapping, and soon the smoke alarm silenced. BeBe had slept through the ruckus.

"Thanks for letting me stay." Perry stretched out on the couch.

"It's not a problem, but shouldn't you have gone home to Mario?"

"Lord, no! He's going to kill me over his car. I need time to formulate a plan. Or an escape route. I'm not sure which. I called and told him the roads were still awful up here."

I tsked.

"Hush now. We all have our methods of self-preservation."

He was right. It was one of the reasons I was here. But I tried not to think about that. Or Daisy's viewing the next day. Or how Kent Ingless might give me nightmares.

I needed to talk to Ian, and to track down Randall Oh as well. He could probably fill in a blank or two.

Bobby came back in, shaking his head. "There were no survivors. There's always cereal."

I thought aloud that a margarita would suffice just fine. Perry agreed and leaned in. "Okay, since I'm here . . . "

"Yeah?" I said.

"We've got to do something about that ponytail."

Thirteen

BeBe slurped me awake early the next morning. I patted the bed next to me and found it empty.

The temperature in Bobby's house had chilled considerably overnight, so I raided his closet once again and came out with a Longhorn sweatshirt.

After a quick brushing of the teeth, wonderful coffee smells lured me into the empty kitchen. The guest bedroom door was closed tight, and I wondered if Perry was going to hide in there all day.

I found Bobby in the living room, typing on a laptop. When I came in, he lowered the screen.

Perching on the edge of the couch, I asked, "What're you working on?"

"It's nothing."

"It's something."

"It's silly."

I rolled my eyes.

He raised the screen. The Word program was open. I read, asked, "What's this?"

"A column."

"Even without my morning caffeine I can see that."

"Mac knows the Lifestyle editor at the *Enquirer*. The paper is looking for a weekly columnist, and Mac gave him my name. And no, the man doesn't owe Mac money."

Mac, Bobby's grandfather, was a geriatric con man, thief, and all-around charmer. I had to admit, my mind had jumped to Bobby's conclusion.

"The editor is looking for an everyday average Joe to write a daily column that's part humor, part social satire, part human interest." He stood, went to the window and looked out. "It's crazy to even think about doing it. My master's is in education administration."

"True, but you are an everyday average Joe, and if you know what social satire is, you're a step ahead of most." I sank into the couch, drew my knees to my chest and pulled my sweatshirt over my legs. My toes stuck out at the hem.

Bobby raised an eyebrow.

"Not quite the same effect as the boxers last night?"

He laughed. "No, but cute all the same."

"Don't make me blush. What about being a principal?"

He shrugged. "I don't know. I've just been out of sorts since Florida. Is it crazy to want to do this?"

"Honestly, yes." I smiled. "But I like crazy."

"That explains a lot."

"It's good," I said, nodding to the computer. It was a humorous piece on men's cooking abilities, featuring the flaming pizzas from last night.

"It's scary."

I knew he wasn't talking about the column. This was a whole shift in his life plan. "I bet."

He paced. "I've got enough saved to try this for a while. Plus, I've really enjoyed playing handyman in the neighborhood. I could do that as a side business. I've plenty of experience painting because of summers working with my family . . ."

"Perry would hire you."

He laughed.

"Sounds like you've made up your mind."

"I guess it does."

"Good for you." I wiggled free of the sweatshirt and gave

him a quick kiss. Smiling, I asked, "This endeavor isn't going to interfere with playing poker today, is it?"

As I drove north to Tam's, I thought about how there shouldn't be blue skies and fifty degree temperatures.

Not today. Maybe not all week.

I was dressed in my only black dress because I was headed straight for the Stangle Funeral Home from Tam's. I even had on panty hose, of which I only owned one pair because I despised them.

My sunglasses slipped down my nose, and I pushed them back up again. All the beautiful snow would soon be gone, and no one had been more upset at the change in the weather than Riley that morning as he skulked out the door to catch the bus to school.

The sun was high in the sky, telling me without looking at my dashboard clock that it was closing in on 10:00 A.M. Daisy's viewing was at noon, at the funeral home back in Freedom.

I wished it was snowing. Or at the very least, raining.

Death called for bad weather, for doom and gloom.

Not sunshine and balmy temperatures.

The theme song for the *Match Game* filled the cab of my truck. I grabbed my cell phone, checked the caller ID, and flipped it open.

"Home yet?" I asked Ana.

"I haven't showered in three days. I think I smell."

I made appropriate clucking noises.

"Don't do that!" Ana said.

"What?"

"Cluck. You sound like Brickhouse. It's freaky."

Oh . . . my . . . God. Was I slowly morphing into a mini-Brickhouse? Clearly, I *was* spending too much time with her. A cutback was in order. Pronto.

"Are you still in Denver?" I asked. I concentrated on the road as I drove, at the cars zipping past me on the highway.

"Dallas." She started humming the theme song of the TV show of the same name. "J.R. was cute, wasn't he?"

"I was more a Bobby fan."

"Go figure. I'm due to land in Cincinnati at three. Can you pick me up?"

"I'll be there."

"Still no sign of Kit?"

I filled her in. Including my latest conversation with Kevin.

"Shot? I feel sick," she said.

"I'm trying not to worry until I talk to Maddie."

In my rearview mirror I caught sight of Lewy and Joe two cars behind me. I sighed.

"When you hear something," Ana said, "text me so I can stop worrying."

"I will."

"Where are you now?"

"I'm off to Tam's to talk to Ian."

"About the little white pills?"

"Yes. Imagine if Daisy was pushing drugs other than the medicinal marijuana? She'd have to have a supplier and less than stellar clients. Any number of them would have motive to kill her. It would also explain the conversation I overheard between her and Kit, about the danger she was in. I wish I'd taken one of the pills with me to show Ian."

"And tamper with a crime scene?"

"Would they have had to know?"

Ana snorted. She'd have definitely taken a pill with her. I was glad she was on her way home, though I worried about Aunt Rosa. "How did your mom take to you leaving?"

"She's pouting, but understands."

This conversation reminded me of Ginger. Had her flight to Wyoming left yet? Had Kevin convinced her that there was nothing going on between the two of us?

Briefly, I wondered why I cared. After all, she was a big part of why my marriage had failed. I should feel zero pity for her. Yet . . . I knew what it was like to question faithfulness in a relationship. I didn't wish it on anyone. Even, dare I say it? Ginger.

"Really?" I finally said once I gathered my thoughts. "Understanding isn't a word I'd use to describe your mom."

"Okay, I had to promise her we'd go on a cruise at Christmastime."

"And?"

"I have to pay for it."

"Small price for Kit?"

"Oh, he's going to owe me, big-time."

I laughed. Understanding wouldn't be a word I'd have used to describe Ana either.

We said our good-byes as I turned into Ian and Tam's driveway.

Ian owned a large farm where he'd once raised English mastiffs, but he gave up breeding dogs once Niki was born. Just not enough time. A lopsided snowman sat melting in the front pasture, missing a charcoal eye. His carrot drooped like a bad nose job, and all but one of his rock buttons had fallen to the ground.

Tam threw open her front door as I stepped out of my truck. She started laughing.

"What's so funny?" I asked, climbing her front steps.

"You! In a dress."

Jeez. "I do, occasionally, wear one."

"Not that I've ever seen. How old is that dress?"

I thought back, lost track. "Old."

"Are those nylons?" Tam asked as she led me into the house.

"Yes, and don't ask how old they are. Hi there, Niki." I crouched down, peeked through the mesh of a playpen and cooed. Niki took one look at me and started wailing. "Why do I always have that effect on her?"

"I'm guessing it's the dress," Tam said, scooping up her daughter.

Niki, at four months, was plump, round, and drooled almost as much as BeBe did. "All right, all right. I'll buy a new dress!"

"Good. I can call Perry and let him know. He apparently saw you leaving this morning and called to warn me."

I wondered if I had Mario's number. It would only be fair to warn him about his precious Saturn.

Tam finally settled Niki just as Ian came in the back door carrying firewood. Niki's whole face lit up. Though Ian wasn't her biological father, I could tell she couldn't care less about DNA.

"Ian told me about the bloodstains and the bullets in the woods by Heavenly Hope," Tam said, nibbling the inside of her cheek.

Ian set the firewood down, began to stack it on the field-stone hearth. "There wasn't a large amount of blood. In all likeliness, the bullet probably grazed the skin."

"But you don't know that for sure," Tam countered.

"And you don't know that Kit was the one hit," Ian said. He tugged off his knit cap, and his blond buzz cut stood on end. "We can't rush to judgments."

Tam looked at me.

I glanced at Ian. "Yes, we can."

He exhaled. "Not you too."

"I'm surprised Kevin didn't warn you."

Ian shook his head and strode to the kitchen to wash his hands.

I leaned into Tam. "I'm going to see Maddie today. I think she may know more about Kit than she's let on. I'm not leaving that funeral home until I know what she knows."

"Which you'll share with law enforcement immediately, right?" Ian stood over my shoulder, hands outstretched for the baby.

Tam passed Niki into his waiting arms.

"When did he become such a fuddy-duddy?" I asked Tam.

"You should have seen him when he caught me searching for information on Heavenly Hope and Daisy online."

"I'm in the room," Ian singsonged.

"Did you find anything?" I asked.

"Nothing."

"You two need—"

"To let the police do their jobs," Tam and I said in unison.

"We know," I said.

"Yet, you carry on."

"Look out your front window."

Ian bounced Niki as he strode to the window, looked out.

"Do you see the Taurus at the gate?"

"Yeah."

"Joe Nickerson and Darren Zalewski. They're the lead investigators on Daisy's case. They've been following me around for the past three days."

Niki gurgled and cooed. Ian's forehead wrinkled.

"See?" I said. "Even you can't explain that one."

"Are you sure they're the lead investigators?"

"That's what they said. I'm sure there are other teams involved, but it's their case. And since it seems as though they're not doing their job, I feel I have to do it for them. Kit's not guilty. He wouldn't hurt anyone. He just wouldn't."

"I agree," Ian said.

That was a relief. Though I wondered if he truly meant it, or if he was just saying so for Tam's benefit.

"I'm hoping you can help me," I said to him, giving him my best Nina puppy dog eyes.

"Oh, good one with the eyes," Tam said. "No one can resist those eyes." She glanced at Ian.

He sighed and sat in a beat-up armchair. "Help with what?"

I told him my theory about Daisy and the drug connection. Ian worked for the DEA and would know about the different types of street drugs. "It was a small pill, white."

"Ian, wouldn't you know if Daisy was pushing drugs?" Tam asked. "She'd have been somewhere on your radar, right?"

Ian shifted in his seat. "Not necessarily. Small white pills? Could be any number of things, from Percocet to Tylenol to migraine medication to fertility drugs."

That narrowed things down.

Niki gazed adoringly up at Ian as he said, "Did it have any markings?"

"There was an image on one side of it, but I couldn't tell what it was."

"Could you sketch it?"

Tam dashed into the kitchen and came back with a pad of paper. I drew what I had seen and passed it to Ian. "Have you ever seen something like that before?"

He nodded. "It's Ecstasy. The street name is Corazón."

"Spanish for heart?" Tam said.

"Look at the image." Ian held up the tablet. "It's a heart. A real heart with valves, aortas, that sort of heart."

Now I knew why it had looked so familiar. I'd recently seen Riley's biology book open to a chapter on heart health.

"Corazón is local to this area. We've been trying to track down the supplier and manufacturer for months now."

"If Daisy was involved in this—" I began.

"Then she was in way over her head," Ian finished. "But right now that's not what I'm most worried about."

The hairs on my neck stood on end. "What is?"

"Because Tam was close to this case, I called in a few favors and asked to see the file. Nina, nowhere in the report does it mention that there were any white pills found next to Daisy's body."

Fourteen

My nylons itched like crazy. I wondered why women put themselves through this kind of torture until I remembered how my legs had looked that morning, a disturbing chalky white. It hadn't taken long for my summer tan to fade.

The things we women did in the name of beauty.

I put on a brave face and strode into Viewing Room 2 at the Stangle Funeral Home. About one hundred people stood elbow-to-elbow in little clusters, the overpowering scent of roses and carnations filling the air.

It was a bit surreal. I hadn't known Daisy in life, and I hadn't really learned anything more about her in death. She was a complete mystery to me. I wanted to stop and question every person I came across, but decided that would be tacky. My mother never would have forgiven me.

I found a quiet corner and pretended to look at the funeral wreaths. I knew being at the funeral home was the perfect place to learn more about Daisy, and possibly more about who wanted her dead, but my mind kept wandering back to Ian and what he'd told me.

No pills had been found with her body.

Had they simply been overlooked or mislabeled? Had BeBe slurped them up when I wasn't looking? I'd seen the way she sucked up doggy kibble . . . had she mistaken the pill for a treat?

That theory didn't make sense. After all, BeBe had been locked in that closet with Daisy for who knew how long. If she hadn't snarfed the pills in that time, why would she have later?

I wondered about a cover-up or possibly dirty police, but that might have been because there was so much talk about corruption in the department over the past six months. The conspiracy theorist in me was hard at work, desperately looking for a link.

Simply because I was desperate.

Daisy had been killed three days ago, and Kit was still the only suspect on the police's radar.

I couldn't believe Creepy Kent hadn't even been a blip.

It didn't seem right.

Thankfully, Ian had promised to look into the missing pills. If anyone could find out what happened to them, it would be Ian.

Especially with Tam nagging him until he did.

Sidestepping, I moved on to another flower arrangement. This one had LOVING DAUGHTER scrolled across a banner draping a wreath made entirely of pink roses.

Dill and Rose stood near the back of the room, greeting people. They were both dressed in black, and both looked as though neither had slept since Friday.

I spotted Kent Ingless standing alone in a far corner, eyes hard, arms folded across his chest. He wore a dark suit and looked more like a Stangle employee than a mourning lover. His expression screamed "Stay away!" Who was I to argue? Okay, I admit the man scared the bejeesus out of me, and you couldn't pay me to wander over to him and offer my condolences.

I had yet to talk with Maddie, who was speaking with a woman near the open casket.

I shuddered.

Dead people gave me the heebies, especially when they

were all dressed up, makeup and hair done as though they were going out for a night on the town instead of spending eternity in a fancy mahogany box with pink satin lining.

Shuddering again, I took a good look around the room. There weren't a lot of people I recognized. How did all of them know Daisy? Family? Friends? Clients?

I skipped from face to face, but I'd yet to see the one person I really wanted to talk to. The one who could hopefully give me some answers as to how entrenched Daisy had been in the drug trade.

Over the din of conversing voices, I heard the vague sound of my cell. People's heads turned as I pulled my phone from my bag.

"Hello," I said, backtracking from the room, making apologies to the mourners at the same time.

"I'm in," Bobby whispered.

"Why are you whispering?"

"I'm literally in."

"Oh!"

"I buddied up with Gus when he made his noontime delivery."

"Where are you now?"

"Bathroom."

I dropped my voice. "So, was I right? About the poker room?"

I edged toward the front doors. One was propped open with a wooden wedge, letting in some air. Thank goodness. It was seriously hot—too many people, too small a room. My nylons felt glued to my legs, which was almost as bad as the wet jean feeling.

"It's a full-fledged operation, Nina. I'm up two hundred bucks."

"Don't get any ideas about playing poker professionally."

He laughed softly. "It does pay well. I've got to go, someone's knocking."

He hung up.

It was nice to have verification on Mrs. Greeble's little hobby, but the question now was, what did I do about it? I'm not sure how the state of Ohio felt about poker clubs. Sure, they were illegal, but to what extent?

And okay, I wasn't so holier-than-thou to care what Mrs. Greeble did in her free time, except Riley was involved.

Which meant I had to be involved too.

And, Lord help me, Kevin.

Trying to come to grips with that bit of depressing news, I turned around and came face-to-face with Kent Ingless, Mr. Creepy himself.

I tried not to jump clear out of my panty hose.

"H-Hello," I said.

His dark eyes narrowed. "You shouldn't be here."

I really didn't like people telling me what I should and shouldn't do. It was why I nearly failed Brickhouse Krauss's tenth grade English class, and it was why I had gone into business for myself. No boss to answer to, though I had to admit, Tam came close, despite the fact that she was my assistant.

"Oh?" I said, since I couldn't come up with anything clever while my stomach was busy twisting itself into knots.

He nudged me toward the door. "You don't get it, do you?"

Outside, I spotted Lewy and Joe sitting in their unmarked. I don't think I was ever happier to see them. Creepy Kent couldn't do much to me without them seeing and hopefully saving me.

I dug in my heels. "Apparently not."

"Go home, Ms. Quinn."

"I can't. I won't." I had people to talk to.

"You can, and you should."

There he went again. I clenched my fists. He'd hit a nerve, and that nerve was twitching to hit back.

"You're scary, I'll give you that," I said. "With those dark eyes and that scowl. And normally, I'd probably be hightailing it away from you, but I came here for a reason, and I'm not leaving until—"

"Nina!" a female voice exclaimed, cutting me off. "I've been looking all over for you!" Maddie pulled me into a fierce hug.

Kent glided away and disappeared into the crowd.

"Is he gone?" she whispered, still holding onto me tight.

"Yes," I squeaked out. "But I . . . can't . . . breathe."

"Oh!" She released me, her dark purple caftan billowing out. "I'm sorry! I saw him out here browbeating you and had to step in. Who was that vile little man?"

The description fit perfectly. "Kent Ingless."

Her dark eyebrows jumped. "Daisy's boyfriend?"

I nodded.

"He's the complete opposite of Kit."

"I'd noticed."

"Do you think Daisy had a split personality?" Maddie asked me, a teasing lilt to her voice.

"Honestly, it's the only thing that makes sense to me. Could you imagine giving up Kit for that?" I asked.

We both shuddered.

"Can I ask you something, Maddie?"

"Sure."

"Is Kit okay? I mean, really okay? I have a feeling he called you. Did he? I think I'm getting an ulcer from worrying about him. Especially now with the bullets and the bloodstains."

The color drained from her face.

Oops. I'd assumed she'd known . . . Suddenly, in my head, I could hear Brickhouse's voice mocking the word *assume*.

"What bullets? What bloodstains?"

I tried to backpedal as I told her what I knew, coloring it in a Pollyanna light.

The color slowly returned to her face. "Come with me."

We ducked into the little girls' room, and Maddie checked under all the stalls for feet. All clear.

Finally, she leaned against a sink and looked me in the eye. "He's called me twice. Once on Friday, once yesterday. Both only for a few seconds. Just enough to tell me he's okay."

Those knots in my stomach started to unravel. He was okay. Thank goodness.

"He didn't mention getting shot."

That either meant he hadn't been shot or he hadn't wanted his mom to worry. Knowing Kit, it was the latter.

"Do you know where he is?" I asked.

"Not a clue. I wish I did. Especially now, knowing he may be injured." She waited a beat, then said, "I trust this information will stay in your confidence?"

"What will?" I asked, looking completely innocent.

She laughed. "I always liked you, Nina."

That meant a lot, especially after Kent's remarks about how Daisy hadn't.

"I hope Kit finds a woman like you someday. Daisy didn't deserve him. Don't get me wrong, she had her good points. But on the whole, she was troubled. Had been since she was a teenager, and didn't want to walk the same line as her parents. They were at their wits' end."

"What happened?" I'd met her parents the other day and hadn't picked up any animosity toward Daisy, except where her dismissal of Kit was concerned.

"Daisy grew up to a certain extent and went to college. She took her business degree and job-hopped for years before opening Heavenly Hope. That's when she started mending her relationship with her parents. Soon after, she started working as a 'freelance therapist' out of the Heavenly Hope office."

"Ahh, the medicinal marijuana."

"Exactly."

"When did Kit meet her?"

"About five years ago." She laughed. "He was one of her clients."

My eyes widened.

"Not for the pot!" She laughed again. "Back then he was into holistic healing and alternative therapies. Or so he says. I think he'd met Daisy beforehand and tracked her down. She is—was—a beautiful girl. However, it didn't take long for him to see that Daisy had issues."

"But he stayed with her anyway? Was it a case of love is blind?"

She shook her head. "It had more to do with him wanting to save her."

"From?"

"Herself."

This explained a lot. Kit did have a tendency to play hero, to rescue damsels in distress. It was a large part of his appeal. The whole Beauty and the Beast syndrome.

The restroom door pushed inward, and an older woman gazed at us with owl-like eyes before rushing into a stall.

Before we were reported to the management for loitering, we left the restroom and headed back toward the crowd in the viewing room. Maddie was asking me about Perry when a bony hand reached out, clamped down on my arm, and wouldn't let go.

Twice. Twice I'd nearly been scared out of my panty hose in one day. That had to be a record.

Thankfully, this time the fear eased the moment I looked at the person who had hold of me. "Pippi!"

She was just the person I wanted to see.

My company, Taken by Surprise, Garden Designs, had done a mini-makeover on Lowther House, a très upscale retirement home, which was owned by Pippi Lowther, a dead ringer for Tweety Bird's cartoon owner.

"Nina, it's good to see you." Pippi's snow white bun wobbled as she kissed each of my cheeks. Several strands of her hair curled softly around her face, and as she turned to introduce herself to Maddie, I saw that the high-necked blouse she wore didn't quite cover the tattoo at the base of her neck.

"Lowther House," I explained to Maddie, "was one of the places Daisy worked as a therapist."

Maddie's eyes widened knowingly.

What she didn't know is that Pippi had taken Daisy's form of therapy to heart and started growing marijuana in a greenhouse in Lowther House's courtyard. That was a secret I'd promised Pippi I'd keep, much to her gratitude.

Just call me Nina Colette Ceceri to Each Her Own Quinn.

"Kit is your son, you say?" Pippi asked.

"He is."

"Lovely boy. Such muscles."

Seemed to me Pippi needed a date.

Maddie smiled but said nothing.

Pippi went on. "Daisy adored him. Spoke well of him always."

We stood to the side of the viewing room door, and people streamed in and out around us. "Yet she broke up with him," I felt the need to mention.

The deep lines around Pippi's eyes crinkled as she frowned. "She said she had her reasons. I didn't know what they were."

"Did she ever speak of Kent Ingless?"

"Who?"

That answered that.

"No one you want to know," I said.

The overhead spotlights picked up the flecks of gold thread running through Maddie's caftan as she waved to someone inside the room. "I'm being summoned. I'll talk to you later, Nina?"

"I'll call if I hear anything," I said.

"Ditto," she called out over her shoulder as she disappeared into the crowd.

Pippi clamped down on my arm again. "She doesn't know about the greenhouse, does she?"

"Not a thing. No one does, as far as I know."

"I can't tell you how grateful I am, how grateful the residents of Lowther House are. Until the government comes to their senses, I'm afraid we're going to have to keep our little secret. Though I must tell you, Nina, dear, I nearly had a heart attack when the police showed up at my door the other day."

"The police?"

"Oh, yes. They wanted to speak to everyone who had anything to do with Daisy. Apparently they had learned of her," she dropped her voice, "alternate therapy."

Amazed that the police had actually been investigating, I leaned against the wall, nearly knocking a framed Thomas Kinkade print clear off.

"They didn't find—"

"No, they didn't search the premises, but I've been proactive. Until this all blows over, I've moved my growing operation to another location."

I thought maybe, just maybe, I ought to give Pippi's name to Ian, then decided against it. Though Ian wasn't above bending the rules from time to time, I couldn't imagine he'd be able to let Pippi's greenhouse thrive.

"Pippi, do you know if Daisy was involved in other forms of alternative therapy? Other illegal forms," I clarified, wiggling my eyebrows for added effect.

"Oh my. Oh dear. Not to my knowledge. Is that possible?"

"It's just a guess at this point."

Her thin lips set. "You ought to speak with Randall."

"Randall Oh?"

"You know him?"

"No. He's on my list of people to talk to."

"It's your lucky day. He's"—she stood on tiptoe—"right over there." She pointed to a young Asian man dressed in a really bad blue suit.

"Could you introduce me?" I asked.

"Sure thing." Throwing bony elbows, she started forward. Over her shoulder she added, "I'm going to miss Daisy."

"What was she like, really like?" I asked. "I keep getting mixed messages."

Pippi slowed to a stop, turned to face me. "Tough as nails. She had a lot of walls built up around her. Beneath the hard exterior, there was a heart of gold. Very few ever saw it, however, because she rarely let her guard down."

The description reminded me a lot of Kit. For the first time I could see what had attracted him to her, besides her natural beauty.

"You either loved her or hated her. There was little in between. Come," Pippi said, clamping onto my arm again. "Oh, and Nina? There's something you should know."

"What's that?"

"Randall and Daisy despised each other." With that she stormed ahead, leaving me in her wake, reeling with the shock of her statement.

Randall Oh zeroed in on us as we neared. I thought I saw a flash of panic sweep through his dark eyes.

Pippi barreled up. "Randall!" She hugged and air-kissed his cheeks. "I'm surprised to see you here."

"Decorum, Pipster."

Pipster? I smiled despite myself. It was a cute nickname.

"I'm not a cruel and heartless bastard, Pips. Just because Daisy and I didn't see eye-to-eye doesn't mean I'm glad she's gone. No one deserves what she got." His hand shot out to mine. "I'm Randall Oh."

He stood an inch or two taller than my five-five and looked to be in decent shape. His hand was clammy.

"Nina Quinn," I said.

"I know. You're my hero. Daisy hated you."

"I've heard," I mumbled.

"Really?" Pippi exclaimed. "Who could hate *you*?"

"I could give you names."

Randall laughed, loud and boisterous. People turned, stared. He covered his mouth and lowered his eyes sheepishly.

"How's Ming these days?" Pippi asked him. "She hasn't been to book club in a while."

"She's fine. Fighting another cold. I think she's milking it. She wants me to move back in with her. As if. I already feel like I'm there more than I am home."

"She is getting older," Pippi said.

"Et tu, Pips?"

She laughed, then poked him with her elbow. "Nina was hoping to have a minute with you, to talk about Daisy. And her, ahem, freelance work."

Part of me wondered why we didn't just come out and say what we were talking about. Seemed to me most people in this room knew the truth.

Again, I saw a smidgen of fear sneak into Randall's eyes as they darted to the exit. It wouldn't be easy to get away, and he must have known it because he said, "Now?"

"If you've got a minute. It won't take long."

He checked his watch, glanced at the casket, shivvied a bit, then said, "Okay."

Pippi led the way to the door, elbows flying. She had the tactic down to a science.

I needed to take notes.

Out in the lobby, she settled onto a wooden bench. Randall sat next to her, his badly cut blue suit pulling tight across his body. He twirled his thumbs as if nervous.

My inner voice asked, *Why?*

I informed it I was going to find out. I kept my voice low as I said, "There's no real delicate way of asking this . . ."

The *Match Game* theme song filled the air. I cursed the timing as I fumbled through my bag.

"Sorry," I said to Pippi and Randall, "it's my son's school."

"Take it, take it," Randall urged, looking pleased over the reprieve.

I answered to find the school nurse on the other end. "Mrs. Quinn, I have Riley here in the clinic."

The faker! He just wanted to get a day off to make up for the lost snow day. I was sure of it.

"He's running a 103 degree temperature, his throat is red, and he has an upset stomach."

Or maybe not.

"Are you available to pick him up, Mrs. Quinn?"

Grr, I hated the *Mrs.* Quinn. I should have gone back to my maiden name after the divorce. Hindsight is evil.

I looked at Randall, at Pippi. I didn't want to leave just yet. But Kevin couldn't drive. Bobby was playing poker. That left my mother or Brickhouse. "Could I call you right back?"

I heard a loud exhale. There went my Stepmother of the Year award. "Fine."

I stepped closer to the outer door, called home. No one answered. I dialed my mother's cell. Again no answer. I called Brickhouse and Mr. Cabrera. No one was there either.

Fabulous.

Snapping my phone closed, I pulled myself together and wandered back over to the bench. "I'm sorry, but I need to leave."

"Nothing serious?" Pippi asked.

"I hope not." To Randall, who looked much relieved, I said, "Could we meet? For coffee?"

"Sure," he agreed, and jotted down his phone number.

I headed for the door and turned to wave good-bye. That's when I saw Kent standing in the viewing room doorway, staring at the three of us, murder in his eyes.

Fifteen

The look in Kent's eyes had chilled me to the bone. I couldn't seem to get warm, no matter how high I turned up my truck's heater.

I took solace in the fact that Lewy and Joe were right behind me, lurking like a dark cloud on a sunny day. Except for a change I was glad to see them. If Kent truly was of a murderous mind, I was safe for the time being.

Or so I hoped.

Lewy and Joe didn't exactly inspire feelings of safety and security.

The roads were wet with melted snow, and the car in front of me kicked up enough water that I flipped on my wipers.

The back and forth motion soothed me as I thought about Daisy and her murder.

I went back to the conversation I'd had with Perry on Saturday. About motives.

Yes, I supposed Kit had a motive, thanks to Kent, but Kit didn't kill Daisy.

He wouldn't. Couldn't.

Now, I could see Kent killing whoever crossed his path. But why? Had he been jealous of Kit? Or . . . Kent had said he met Daisy through work. His or hers?

Suddenly I wondered if they were one and the same.

Kent had said, "I'm a chef of sorts."

Suddenly, something Ian said popped into my head. *Corazón is local to this area. We've been trying to track down the supplier and manufacturer for months now.*

Was it possible Kent was the manufacturer?

I quickly called Tam and asked a huge favor. One I hoped she didn't share with Ian.

She agreed and promised to get back to me within an hour.

I thought again about what Kent had said about Daisy. About how she'd been killed doing what she thought was right.

What *she* thought. Not what *was* right.

If—and it was just speculation at this point—Daisy wanted out of the drug business, and Kent manufactured the Ecstasy Daisy doled out, then he'd have plenty of motive to kill her.

My one problem with that theory was that I believed him when he said he'd loved her. Would he have chosen money over love? Was he that ruthless?

The answer was a quick yes.

I didn't rule out Randall Oh's involvement either. I had a lot of questions I wanted to ask him. If he'd truly worked closely with Daisy, he would know all her secrets. He'd know for certain if she was dabbling in other illegal drugs. He'd know if Kent Ingless was her supplier. He'd know who might have a motive for killing her.

I couldn't forget that Randall and Daisy had been enemies. What had caused a rift between the two?

One thing I knew for sure: It would be foolhardy for me to meet with him alone. As of now, everyone was a suspect in my mind. Just because my first impression of Randall had been a good one didn't mean I should trust my instincts.

As I knew quite well, my instincts were often wrong.

Dead wrong.

I pulled up in front of Riley's high school and walked into the office to sign in. A weird sense of déjà vu came over me. This is where I'd first met Bobby, when he was Riley's principal. It seemed like a lifetime ago, yet it had only been seven months.

So much had changed.

"Do you know where the clinic is?" the receptionist asked.

I didn't recognize her, and was glad Bobby wasn't working there anymore, as she was young and cute and curvy in all the right places.

A girl could get seriously jealous.

"Yes, thanks."

I backtracked out of the office and walked into the clinic just in time to see Riley bend over and toss his cookies into a bedpan.

My stomach heaved.

I'd never been good with cookie-tossing.

The nurse wore a look on her face that told me she truly was the best person for her job. It was a mix of compassion and sympathy as she offered Riley a cool towel.

They both looked up at me, and the nurse had me sit immediately, worried about the lack of color in my face.

"I'm all right." I rose after a minute or two, testing my legs. "Thanks."

"You look worse than me, Nina," Riley said.

"Nina?" said the nurse, returning from rinsing Riley's pan. "This isn't your mom?"

I sat back down. There was only so much I could take in one day.

"Stepmom," Riley mumbled.

"Oh," the nurse said. "That makes sense. I was thinking you were too young to have a son Riley's age."

I wanted to lean over and kiss her. I might have to make her my new best friend. I was sure Ana wouldn't mind.

"You just made my day. And trust me, it needed to be made. You ready?" I asked Riley.

"What's with the dress?" he asked. "Is that Grandma Cel's? No, can't be. She has better taste."

The nurse snickered.

Suddenly, she was off my list for new best friend.

I stood again. "You're awfully chatty for someone so sick."

"You need to burn that thing, Nina," he said, wobbling to his feet.

"So I've heard." I took hold of his arm. Amazingly, he didn't pull away.

"You better take this." The nurse handed over the bedpan. "Just in case."

"You're not going to get sick in my truck, are you?" I asked, feeling the color drain from my face.

"Depends."

"On?"

"Whether you start driving like Maria or Ana." Maria, my sister, was a notoriously bad driver. And Ana was worse.

"I'll do my best." I tried not to notice how his hot skin scorched my fingers. "Do you have a coat?"

"No."

"A hat?"

"No."

"Gloves?" I ventured.

"No."

"No wonder you're sick."

"I'm a man," he said in a boastful voice. "I don't need no coat."

"No, just tutoring from Brickhouse."

"If I wasn't so sick, I'd give you attitude."

"Wait. Let me count my blessings." I helped him into the truck, thrust the pan at him.

There was no sign of Lewy and Joe. Wonder where they'd snuck off to?

"So, really, why the dress?" Ry asked once I set the truck into gear.

"Daisy's viewing."

When he didn't say anything else, I glanced over at him.

His lips were rough around the edges and had turned a dark red, something that happened every time he had a fever.

Poor kid. "You okay?"

"Do I look it?" he snapped.

"Whoa, what happened to no attitude?"

"I lied."

His mood swing shouldn't have taken me by surprise, but it did.

The silence stretched. It wasn't uncomfortable, yet I felt as though there was a bit of tension in the air. I couldn't figure out where it stemmed from until Riley said, "All Kit was doing was trying to help her, and this is the thanks he gets."

Ah.

Riley and Kit had become best buds since Kit moved in with us. Riley looked up to him, and I was glad for the role model. Kit was hardworking, loyal, and an all-around good man. His appearance fooled many people, but those who took the time, treasured the man beneath the scary surface.

Riley had taken the time.

"He'll be okay," I said.

"How do you know?"

"Faith. Faith that good triumphs over evil."

He rolled his eyes. "That makes me want to throw up again."

"Just not in my truck, okay? And it's true, whether it's hokey or not."

"It's hokey."

I took a deep breath. Dealing with a teenager took special skills. One of them was deep cleansing breaths. It was the only way to get through a conversation.

I was on breath number six when what Riley had said sunk in. "Do you know what Kit was doing to help Daisy?"

Kit and Riley spent a lot of time together, and Riley was sneaky. He could have seen or heard specifics.

Riley shrugged. He had it down to an art form.

"If you know anything, Riley, you should tell me. Kit needs all the help he can get right now."

"I don't know much."

Not wanting to push, I kept quiet.

A minute went by. I could tell he was wrestling with being loyal to Kit and trying to help him at the same time. Finally he said, "Kit told me that sometimes it's important to help people even when they don't want the help."

"That's true."

"I overheard one of their conversations once. About how Daisy was in danger. She kept saying that if he helped her, he'd be in danger too."

Sounded similar to the conversation I'd overheard between the two.

"Daisy wanted to do it on her own."

"Do what?"

"I don't know. It had something to do with some guy named Kent, and about someone named Cora?" He said this last part as a question, as if he wasn't quite sure.

"Corazón?" I repeated.

"Yeah, that's it. I remember now because it reminded me of Corona beer."

I shot him a look.

"What? I watch TV."

Great. Now I was going to have to lock up all the liquor in the house.

"Kit knew I'd been listening. Told me not to tell anyone what I'd heard."

"I'm sure he doesn't mind you telling me."

He said nothing.

I wanted to feel him out, see exactly how much he knew. "Listen, do you know what Daisy and Kit were talking about? With the Corazón?"

He shook his head. "All I kept thinking about was beer."

Yep. Definitely locking up the alcohol.

This stepmothering thing wasn't as easy as it seemed.

"Corazón is Spanish for heart," I said. "And it's also a type of Ecstasy."

As he looked at me his lips flamed, his face paled. "I don't understand," he said. "What's Corazón have to do with Kit and Daisy?"

"I don't know." Kent's murderous glare came to mind. "But I intend to find out."

I turned onto my street and slowed as I neared my house. A large group of people had gathered on my driveway.

What now?

I pulled into Bobby's driveway since mine was completely blocked. County vehicles were parked at my curb, and I saw a reporter for the local paper snapping random pictures.

Riley groaned.

Or maybe it was me.

I wasn't sure.

Riley shook off my help crossing the street. He clutched his bedpan for dear life.

I cozied up to Flash, who stood on the outskirts of the crowd along with Miss Maisie. "What's going on?"

"Donatelli went and caught himself one of those turkeys," Flash said, not even looking at me.

Miss Maisie leaned across him. "The county is here to take it away, and that horrid little rooster too."

Riley swayed, and I grabbed hold of him. "You okay?" I asked him.

"Can you help me inside?"

"What's wrong with the boy?" Flash asked.

Stepping toward the house, I said, "He's sick."

Miss Maisie let out a shriek. "He's got it! I know he has. He's got the bird flu! Probably from trying to catch that contaminated rooster!"

The crowd quieted and everyone turned our way. The newspaper guy snapped three pictures.

This time I was positive it was Riley who moaned.

"Chérie!" My mother rushed over. "What's wrong with Riley?"

"Riley?" Kevin piped in, joining us.

"Kill me now," Riley mumbled.

"He's sick," I said. "The school called."

"Why didn't they call here?" Kevin asked.

"They did. No one answered." I made a show of looking around at the crowd. "Seems you all were busy doing other things."

"Is it really the bird flu?" the reporter asked.

"Idiot," Riley mumbled.

I agreed.

As it was, Miss Maisie was already hobbling across the street as fast as her legs could carry her. No doubt there would be garlic over her door by sundown, just in case.

"Come on," I said, throwing elbows as I'd seen Pippi do. Only my elbows didn't seem to work as well.

Thank goodness Brickhouse stepped in and cleared a path for us to the door. "Ach, I'll make you some nice chicken soup."

"No!" Riley said. "No chicken. No turkey."

"Ach. Split pea."

"You should have taken the chicken," I whispered, pushing him inside. "I'll be a minute."

"What's wrong with him?" Brickhouse asked me as soon as I closed the door behind Riley.

"Flu, maybe."

"Ach! I have yet to get my flu shot."

"I haven't had mine either," my mother said, coming up behind me.

Kevin finally made it to the porch. "Is he all right?"

"Some sort of flu," I said. "It's probably best you not go near him right now. If you catch what he has, it will probably send you back to the hospital."

Wait. Would that be such a bad thing?

Hmmm.

Okay, I wasn't that heartless. It would be bad.

Worry knitted Kevin's brow. "Should I call his pediatrician?"

"Why don't we wait until tomorrow? See how he does tonight. Maybe it's a twenty-four-hour bug. What's the deal here?" I asked, motioning to the crowd.

Kevin sat on the porch railing. "The county is just loading the birds on the truck now. The SPCA promised to come later to catch the other turkey."

As I watched Mr. Cabrera speaking with the reporter and posing for pictures, Lewy and Joe pulled up across the street.

They both got out of their car holding Starbucks cups. No wonder they weren't right behind me on the way home. It had been snack time.

The crowd cleared when the county trucks pulled away. My mother went inside to make Riley some tea, and Brickhouse waddled off to make soup.

"Isn't that the dress you wore to my mother's funeral seven years ago?" Kevin asked.

"So?"

"Just saying."

Hmmph.

"And, you know, I haven't forgotten that you need to explain why you were searching Riley's room."

"I told you, I was cleaning."

"Nina . . . "

Lewy and Joe climbed the steps to the porch and greeted Kevin with nods. "Looks like we missed the circus," Lewy said.

I placed my hand on the doorknob. "You can read about it in the paper."

"Before you go . . . " Lewy started.

"Yeah?"

"The Georgia State Patrol has come up with no leads on Kit. The guys we sent down have hit dead ends too."

I didn't know what to say, so I said nothing.

"Here," Joe said, handing me a piece of paper.

"What's this?"

"The number for the impound lot." Joe smirked. "It's going to cost you a pretty penny to get your truck back."

"Not as much as the taxpayers will have spent for the wild goose chase you masterminded." Lewy sipped his coffee, eyebrows raised.

He was baiting, but I wasn't biting. "I'm too tired to play these games with you two."

I walked inside. As I closed the door I heard Joe say to Kevin, "It was worth a try."

Yeah, well. He could keep on trying.

Upstairs, I found Riley snuggled into his bed, already asleep.

Xena was snoozing too. Thank goodness.

"*Chérie*, here's his tea," my mother said from the doorway.

"You can come in."

"No thank you."

I smiled. My mother and germs had never gotten along.

I took the tray. A small bottle of ibuprofen sat alongside a steaming mug and a bottle of water.

Shaking gently, I woke Riley long enough for him to swallow two pills. I pulled his desk chair over next to the bed and sat, sipping on his tea.

Lost in thought, it took me a good minute to realize my mother was calling me from downstairs.

I went to the door. "Yes?"

"You've another patient, *chérie*! He needs help up the stairs!"

The scent of Lysol filled the hallway. My mother was already at work degerminating.

At the bottom of the steps, Perry drooped piteously.

"I don't feel well, Nina."

"You don't look good, Perry."

"Can I stay here?"

My mother chimed in. "Kevin is helping Flash bring a cot over from his house for Perry to use."

"Let's get you upstairs," I said to Perry, since my mother had clearly made the decision already.

It took a good fifteen minutes for me to get the cot set up in Riley's room, to hunt down a sleeping bag, and to get Perry settled. I'd given him the same therapy as Riley. Two ibuprofen, a pillow, and a bedpan as a woobie.

"Thank you, Nina," Perry whispered.

I pulled one of Riley's shades down and then crossed to the other window. "What are friends for?"

"Another pillow?" he asked.

I laughed as I reached for the shade pull. "Uh-oh."

"What?" he squawked.

"You're about to feel a lot worse."

"Why?"

"Mario just pulled up."

Sixteen

Mario stormed into the house, ranting and raving about a phone call he'd gotten from a tow truck driver.

By the time he made it upstairs, his mocha skin had turned a mottled raspberry. I worried for his health as I stood in front of Perry, bound and determined to protect him as best I could.

But one look at Perry, and Mario seemed to forget why he was angry.

He crouched down beside the cot and started rambling something softly in Spanish that I couldn't understand but made me wish Bobby spoke the language.

The cooing went on for a good ten minutes before Mario decided he wanted to take Perry home.

"Are you sure?" I asked. "I don't mind watching over him. Riley's already sick . . . "

Mario helped Perry sit up. "He should be home in his own bed."

"Oooh, my feather bed," Perry cooed.

Riley rolled over in his sleep, mumbling, "Gobble, gobble."

Mario eyed him, then me. "Hallucinating?"

"Long story," I told him. "Perry can fill you in." I gave them both hugs and told them to call if they needed anything.

"Do you happen to know where my car is?" Mario asked.

Perry moaned, holding his stomach.

Mario again cooed something in Spanish, this time with a touch of an evil tone that made me wonder if it was some sort of hex.

When they'd left, I remade the cot and changed the pillowcase just in case another victim showed up. My cell phone rang, and I answered before it finished the first ring. It was Tam.

She was whispering. "Kent Ingless graduated with a degree in chemistry. He worked at a biomedical firm for twenty years before dropping off the radar. Does that tell you anything?"

"Yeah, it does." I told her my theory about Kent being the creator of Corazón.

"A mad scientist," she said.

"Something like that."

"Should I tell Ian?"

"Let me," I said. "I don't want him mad at you."

We said our good-byes just as Bobby strode into Riley's room. He wore dark jeans, a long-sleeve thermal tee that matched his blue eyes, and a big smile.

"I won three hundred dollars," he said, kissing me.

"Don't get used to it."

"Spoilsport," he teased. "How's Ry?"

"Not good. He's dreaming about turkeys." I plopped down in the chair, set my feet on the bed.

Bobby perched on the edge of the desk. "A sixteen-year-old dreaming about turkeys? He must be really sick."

"I'm hoping it's a twenty-four-hour bug, for his sake." I looked up at him. "How'd this afternoon go, besides the big windfall?"

"I didn't get much out of the crowd at Mrs. Greeble's. I did gather there's been a game going on for about three months now."

"Does Mrs. Greeble play? Or deal?"

"No, she just sits in a rocker in the corner and watches some, but mostly nods off. And honestly, she doesn't look so well. I wonder if she has whatever Riley has."

It wouldn't have surprised me, seeing as how much time they spent together.

I crossed my feet at the ankles. Big fluffy socks covered my toes, keeping them warm. "I'm surprised Mrs. Greeble allowed you to play. She must know you'd tell me about it."

"She didn't seem to notice I was there."

That didn't sound like her at all. Usually she was as sharp as they came, often giving Mr. Cabrera what-for because of his snooping.

Great. Now I was worried about her as well.

That was me. Nina Colette Ceceri Worrywart Quinn.

Sometimes, just sometimes, my empathy for others bothered me. Now was one of those times.

Bobby's cell phone rang, and he frowned at the readout. "Robert MacKenna," he said, answering.

Once again I had a flash of déjà vu. I'd known him by that name when he was Riley's vice principal. It wasn't until we'd gotten closer that I started calling him Bobby.

Bobby fit much better, I thought, looking at him. It was looser, and better represented his easygoing personality. As he leaned over, listening to whoever was on the line, his body moved with an athletic grace. Toned muscles strained his long-sleeve tee, and the cut of his jeans hinted at the long, strong legs beneath.

He didn't belong behind a desk. His happiness and eagerness to do something new shone in his eyes. And I had to admit that I was glad he was venturing into a new career. I liked seeing him this way.

"I'll be right over," he said, hanging up.

"Not more poker?" I asked.

He laughed. "Mrs. Daasch. Her kitchen sink won't drain."

Riley shifted again. "Gobble, gobble."

Bobby grinned. "Must really be some dream."

"I was the one chased by those turkeys." I smiled. "I should be the one having nightmares."

Laughing, he leaned down next to my chair and softly kissed my lips. Looking into my eyes, he said, "You're staying with Riley tonight?"

I loved when he looked at me like that. All warm and understanding. My heart swelled. I nodded.

He kissed me again. "Try to stay out of trouble."

"Me? Trouble? Ha!"

He managed to laugh and look skeptical at the same time. "I'll see you tomorrow." He stopped in the doorway, looked back at me.

"All right," I said.

After a long moment, he left.

I sat there nibbling my lip. I should have said it.

I love you.

"Why don't you just tell him you love him and get it over with? I didn't think he was ever going to leave. Poor guy," Riley said, his voice scratchy.

I stuck a straw in the bottle of water and held it to his lips. "Why poor guy?"

Riley shifted in bed, pulling the covers up to his chin. His lips were still bright red and chapped. The fever hadn't broken.

"It's obvious that he loves you and is afraid to say it because he doesn't know if you'll say it back."

"When did you become Dr. Phil?"

"Get a clue, Nina."

Just how did Riley know that I hadn't told Bobby I loved him? That we didn't say it all the time to each other? I needed to stop underestimating how mature teenagers were. Immediately, I added it to my personal commandment list.

Bobby and I had danced around the words for over a month now. And Riley was right. I could tell Bobby was scared to lay it on the line. And for some reason, I was scared to put it out there. It was stupid. Really stupid. And immature. I mean, why not just say it? I felt it. I think he felt it. Yet . . .

"You two make me feel sicker. How about you keep your lovey-dovey stuff out of my room?"

Downstairs, I heard commotion. A second later I heard Brickhouse's loud voice carrying on about the wonders of split pea soup.

Ahh, sweet revenge for his smart mouth! "Sounds like your dinner has arrived, Ry."

"Don't make me eat it," he muttered piteously.

"You should have thought about that before the lovey-dovey comment."

"Dammit," he said.

"Language!"

He pulled the covers over his head as Mr. Cabrera poked his head in the door like a turtle out from its shell. "Soup's on!" He passed in a covered Tupperware dish with a spoon balanced on top. "There's more downstairs if you're hungry," he said to me.

"I'll pass," I said, taking the dish and lifting the lid off.

He frowned. "Don't go hurtin' Ursula's feelings."

"I wouldn't dream of it."

Riley snorted.

"You doin' okay, kid?" Mr. Cabrera asked.

Riley's voice was muffled, coming through the comforter. "Just fine."

"That's a boy. Can't keep the good ones down long. We'll be downstairs if you change your mind, Miz Quinn."

"Thanks," I said, knowing perfectly well there was no way on earth I was eating split pea soup.

I set the bowl on Riley's nightstand. "Looks delish," I said.

He groaned.

I smiled.

My cell phone rang, the *Match Game* theme song filling the air.

Ana.

Oh no. Ana!

"Hello?" I answered cautiously.

"You forgot about me!" she cried.

"No, no, I didn't," I lied, grimacing.

"Then where might you be?" she asked.

"Well, you see, Riley's sick—"

"You forgot about me!"

Crap. I couldn't leave Riley. No one else would step foot into his room except for Bobby, and he was off fixing Mrs. Daasch's drain.

I looked at the lump that was Riley under the covers. He would probably be just fine by himself. He was, after all, sixteen, not six. But I didn't feel right leaving him.

"Someone will be there in half an hour." That was pushing it. The airport was easily forty-five minutes away.

"Someone?"

"I told you, Riley's sick."

"I'm not a baby," floated out from under the covers.

"I thought you were making that up! What's wrong?" Ana asked.

"Some sort of flu. Fever, cookie-tossing—"

"Don't remind me," Riley moaned. "The smell of the soup is making my stomach turn."

I grabbed the bowl, clicked on the lid, and set it in the hall. Like I said, I didn't do well with cookie-tossing.

"Fine," Ana said. "Just send someone."

She hung up, and I went in search of Mr. Cabrera. It didn't take much for him to agree to pick up Ana—they had become fast friends over the last few months. Besides, I had a hunch he didn't like the soup very much and wanted the excuse to abandon supper.

I grabbed a cup of coffee and headed back upstairs. Riley had fallen asleep again.

Sinking into the chair, I stared into my mug. The dark coffee jarred my memory.

In my room, I dug Randall Oh's phone number out of

my purse. Hoping we could have coffee first thing in the morning, I dialed.

Two rings later a tinny voice came on the line telling me the number I dialed was not in service.

I redialed carefully, just to be sure.

No doubt about it. Randall Oh had given me a fake number.

It made me wonder why.

Seventeen

I woke to the sun streaming in my bedroom window and someone's hand under my camisole, rubbing my back in lazy, sensuous circles.

I knew that hand, that touch.

And didn't like it. Not one bit.

Jumping up, I grabbed my duvet, covering myself to my neck. "Get out!"

Kevin propped himself up on his elbow. My yanking of the covers revealed him to be shirtless with nothing on but jammie bottoms and gauze covering the wound near his collarbone. "Why? I was just getting started."

My temper flared.

Then . . .

I smiled.

"That's better." Kevin reached for me.

I slapped his hand.

"Ow! What was that for?"

"Don't touch me."

He sat up. "Why the smile then? Talk about mixed messages."

"I just realized something."

"Do share," he mocked.

"Your touch didn't affect me. In fact, I didn't like it. Don't you see? I'm over you. Really over you. I love Bobby. It was his touch I was hoping for when I opened my eyes."

Looking wounded, he said, "Let me get this knife out of my heart, and I'll get out of your way."

My anger slowly returned. "Wait. Where do you get off?" I asked. "What were your intentions coming in here?"

He laughed. "I thought that was obvious."

My hands shook I was so mad. "I don't get you. I really don't. I can't believe I'm about to say this, Lord help me because I must have caught Riley's illness and be nearly delusional, but I feel bad for Ginger. Did you think about her at all when you climbed into my bed this morning?"

His eyes darkened.

"You're supposed to be committed to her, and here you are sneaking into my bed like a sneaky, no-good, low-down, dirty—"

"We broke up," he interrupted.

"—snake," I finished. "What?"

"We broke up. Yesterday."

"Why?"

He shrugged, and pain flitted across his face. My gaze shot to the scars on his chest, but there was no way I was offering him sympathy now, not a single chance, no way in— "You okay?"

"Fine."

"Fine."

A prime example of our primo communication skills.

"I just thought," he said.

I stood up, wrapping my duvet around me. "I know what you thought. You figured that since Ginger was out of the picture you could slide right back into mine because you knew I still had feelings for you, deep down. You figured I'd sleep with you, realize what I'd been missing, and come running back with open arms. You know what?"

"I don't think I want to know."

"You figured wrong. I don't have feelings, deep down. They're gone. I deserve better than you, Kevin. *I* deserve a man who loves *me* for all the right reasons. And though I hate her, Ginger deserves a man to love her the same way. You know what?"

"I still think I don't want to know."

"I think you still love Leah."

His eyes flashed, burning green.

"Yeah, I said it. You still love Leah. And I don't think it was fair to me, or to Ginger, that you had relationships with us without fully being able to commit." My voice softened, my heart suddenly breaking for him. "And you won't ever be able to have a relationship with a woman until you're able to fully put Leah to rest. In your mind. In your heart. You haven't allowed yourself to do that, Kevin. You need to. For your sake. For your happiness."

He pulled both hands down his face. "Yeah," was all he said as he walked out of my room.

Taking a deep breath, I sat down on the edge of my bed, wrapping my duvet around me like a cocoon. Tears hovered at the corners of my eyes and I wasn't sure why. I couldn't nail down a single one of the many emotions coursing through me.

Riley appeared in the doorway, like the ghost of Christmas past. Pale, wide, watery eyes, red lips, wild hair. Just give the boy some chains to rattle and he'd be a dead ringer.

"Are you all right?" I asked him. "Do you need something?" I'd spent most of the night in his room, dozing in his chair, holding his bedpan for him while he was sick. I personally thought it was enough for my Stepmother of the Year nomination to be reinstated, especially after being in such close proximity to Xena all night. Though, I confess, I'd thrown a sheet over her cage to help ward off the heebies. I hadn't crept into my bed with my mother and BeBe—who was so happy to see me she nearly knocked my mother out of bed with her tail—until nearly four in the morning. It was close to nine now. No sign of Mom or BeBe.

"I'm okay. You?" he asked me.

It dawned on me that he'd overheard.

Crap.

"Yeah. Sorry you heard all that."

Slowly, he came into the room, sat on the bed next to me. He was such a mirror of his father. Yet, he was so different than Kevin. Softer, despite the attitude. Wiser, despite his age. In his eyes I could see the man he would become. The good man. It did my heart proud.

He gazed at me, saying nothing.

I let out a deep breath, not sure what to say either.

Finally, in a raspy voice, he said, "Do you need a hug?"

Slowly, I nodded.

He wrapped me in his arms, cocoon and all, and I couldn't keep the tears from falling.

A minute later my mother walked into the room and gasped. "What's going on? Did someone die?"

Riley backed away, and I noticed moisture in his eyes too. I wiped away my tears. "No. But I think we're all mourning something this morning." I shooed Riley off my bed. "Go lie down. I'll bring you some medicine in a minute."

He left, walking slowly, as if the fever wouldn't let him move any faster. My mother took his place on the bed.

Her eyes were filled with tears.

"Why are you crying?" I asked her.

"Mothers, *chérie*, will always cry when they see their babies in pain."

She put an arm around me. I dropped my head onto her shoulder and told her about my conversation with Kevin.

"It was something he needed to hear, *chérie*. And it was very brave of you to tell him so."

"I love Bobby," I said to her.

"I know that, *bébé*."

I looked into her eyes, a blue much like Riley's. "Then why do I feel guilty for not loving Kevin anymore?"

"Because, you're a fixer. Fixers want everyone to be happy. It's time for you to learn, perhaps, that sometimes people need to fix themselves."

"It sucks." I sniffled.

She laughed. "That it does. Get dressed. I'll make you some breakfast." My mother thought food was the best medicine for any ailment. "Remember, I'm taking Kevin for his checkup this afternoon, so we'll be gone for a trifle."

The house almost to myself . . . It was enough to make me giddy.

I took a few minutes to get dressed, brush my hair, my teeth. I still felt out of sorts with myself and thought talking to Ana about it would make me feel better.

She didn't answer her home number. I tried her cell next, but it went straight to voice mail.

I hadn't heard from her last night, but figured she'd been pouting about being left at the airport. Was she still mad at me?

I dialed Riley's pediatrician next and made an appointment.

While I had the phone out, I called Tam to do a little research for me and asked to speak to Ian.

"He's not here, Nina."

"Oh. I was hoping to talk to him."

"You could call his cell, but if you just wait you should see him today."

"I should?"

"I know he was planning to stop by your house today. To see you."

By the time I made it downstairs, no one was around. I peeked out the kitchen window and saw why. All hell was breaking loose outside.

I rushed out the back door and into the fray. I spotted Brickhouse on the fringe, BeBe at her feet, sitting obediently. She licked my hand as I sidled up, trying to take it all in, pick apart conversations.

I spotted the local reporter milling around the crowd, and soon a news van pulled up in front of Miss Maisie's house.

"What's going on?" I asked.

She clucked. "Twenty frozen Cornish game hens were delivered all throughout the neighborhood this morning to various residents. Miss Maisie is convinced someone is trying to poison the elderly neighbors, and she called the news."

Miss Maisie needed meds.

But . . . who on earth would send Cornish game hens? It had to have something to do with the turkeys and Gregory Peck as well.

"Who delivered the hens?"

"UPS."

I laughed. I couldn't help it. Brickhouse cracked a smile too. BeBe's tail swished.

We watched the crowd. People circled, traveling from one conversation to another. My mother, Kevin, Mr. Cabrera, Flash, and even Bobby were in the midst of it all.

There was no sign of Ian. I wondered when he might be coming by and what he needed to see me about. Had he found out anything on the missing white pills?

Brickhouse clucked. "UPS can track the buyer."

"Unless they used a fake name."

"You always were a killjoy, Nina Ceceri."

As I smiled—it was such fun bantering with Brickhouse—I spotted Miss Maisie storm into her house and slam the door. A second later Bobby walked over to us. I gave him a kiss. "What's with Miss Maisie?"

"Someone suggested a huge bonfire to roast the hens, and she stormed off. She's still convinced someone is trying to spread the bird flu through the Mill. You okay?" he asked me, looking closely at my eyes. "Rough night?"

Rougher morning, I thought, but I simply nodded.

He put his arm around me, tucked me close to his body. I felt like I could stay there the rest of the week.

Mr. Cabrera wandered over, throwing his hands in the air. "That Maisie is a loony toon!"

"Donatelli!" Brickhouse admonished.

"What?" he asked. "It's true."

"Be that as it may, be nice."

I smiled. They were good for each other.

"I don't know what people are complainin' about," he grumbled. "You'd think they'd be grateful for somethin' to put on their dinner table. Those hens aren't cheap." He caught my eye. "Miz Quinn, you don't look so good. You catch that flu?"

I made a mental note to apply more makeup once I went back inside. "I'm fine. Thanks."

"The boy?"

"Going to the doctor in a little bit."

"Good, good. That doc of his will fix him up good."

My mind played mental association. Mr. Cabrera mentioning the doctor reminded me of Ana's dalliance with Johan, Dr. Feelgood, which reminded me that I hadn't been able to get hold of my cousin that morning. "Thanks for picking up Ana yesterday," I said.

"No problem, Miz Quinn. Miz Ana is a hot ticket."

Brickhouse elbowed him.

"Not as hot as you," he said to her.

I felt Bobby's chest vibrate as he laughed.

"Did she get home okay?" I asked.

"You sayin' somethin' about my drivin'?" Mr. Cabrera looked put out.

"Not at all. I just haven't been able to reach her this morning."

"I dropped her off at her front door. She didn't want me to come up. I waited till she got in, then drove off."

Something just didn't feel right. Ana might have been mad at me, but she'd still want to help Kit. I made a mental note to call her again once I reapplied more makeup. Priorities.

An SPCA truck pulled up to the crowd, and right behind it, Joe and Lewy's dark Ford pulled into my driveway. They got out, zeroed in on me immediately, their faces grim.

"What now?" I asked aloud.

Brickhouse clucked. I noticed she loosened BeBe's leash just enough so BeBe could launch herself at someone if need be.

Honestly, I thought I must have been sick or something, because Brickhouse was definitely growing on me.

Kevin strode over when he saw Joe and Lewy approaching. He wouldn't look at me.

"What's wrong?" I asked the detectives once they were close enough. "It's not Kit, is it? Is he okay?"

"No idea," Joe said.

Then I couldn't imagine what would warrant such long faces.

"You've got news?" Kevin asked.

"There's been another murder," Lewy said.

My stomach fell. Bobby tightened his arm around me.

"Who?" Kevin asked.

"Kent Ingless. He was found shot at close range early this morning."

Eighteen

"I can't say I'm glad to see him gone," Brickhouse said an hour later.

BeBe had gone upstairs, where she now slept at the foot of Riley's bed.

I set the kettle on the stove. "Me either, but you know they'll think Kit did it."

I peeked in the fridge. Nearly empty. Great.

Thanksgiving was in two days, and I didn't even have a turkey yet. Some impression I was going to make on Bobby's family.

I pulled out a box of stale Nilla Wafers from the cupboard and set them on the counter. Desperate times and all.

Apparently I had issues with cutting back on Brickhouse time, because it had been me who invited her in for tea. There weren't enough corners in my head to tuck away that information.

My father, looking well-rested, had dropped a car off for my mother. Mr. Cabrera had volunteered to drive him home, since for some reason Dad didn't feel like hanging out with us.

Hmm. Empty house, full fridge, peace and quiet.

Couldn't imagine why he chose to go home.

My mother had taken Kevin to his doctor's appointment

downtown, promising me in a hushed whisper to get the full scoop on Kevin and Ginger's breakup.

Bobby was off fixing another leak of Mrs. Daasch's, and I was beginning to suspect she was breaking things on purpose.

Ana still wasn't answering her phone. Part of me wondered if she'd met a man on the plane and made other plans.

But then the reality sank in. She was honestly worried about Kit. So where was she?

"With Kent dead," I said, "there goes my prime suspect."

"Ach. Mine too."

I filled her in about Randall Oh. "He did give me a fake number, so obviously he's trying to avoid me. Why?"

"Because you're annoying?"

"And here I was sharing my Nilla Wafers with you."

"Ach. They're stale."

I grit my teeth and returned to the conversation. "Maybe Randall is the killer. Maybe he killed Daisy because he's selling drugs too, and wanted the business all for himself."

"Then why kill Mr. Creepy if he was the supplier?"

"Okay, maybe Randall killed Daisy because he knew Daisy was dealing and it hurt his reputation? Killing Creepy Kent then makes sense, if Randall wanted to eliminate all the drug influences surrounding Heavenly Hope."

"Did you tell the detectives these theories?"

The teapot whistled. I poured water into two mugs. Cocoa for me, tea for Brickhouse. "Actually, I did."

"And?"

"They laughed."

She clucked.

"But they did promise to look into Randall."

Not that I had any faith whatsoever they would. I added a heaping mound of whipped cream to my cocoa, and Brickhouse added a touch of milk to her tea.

We sipped in silence until the doorbell rang. I heard excited barking from upstairs, then silence. Riley seemed to have a magic touch with BeBe that I lacked.

Peeking out the front window, my eyes widened. I pulled open the door.

"Hello, Nina."

"Mrs. Greeble. Come in."

Pain creased her features with each of her steps. I automatically took her arm, led her to the kitchen and into a chair at the table. "Would you like some tea?"

She shook her head.

"Coffee?"

Again, no.

"Cocoa?"

Her watery eyes lit. "That would be lovely."

Her cheeks drooped and her skin had a yellowish, unhealthy undertone.

Bobby was right. She didn't look well.

"I came," she said, "to see how Riley was feeling."

Brickhouse levered herself off the counter stool and sat across from Mrs. Greeble at the table. "Not so good," she said.

"Certainly not the bird flu, as Maisie is telling everyone?"

"No," I said. "Just some sort of flu."

She nodded.

The teapot whistled quickly, the water still fairly hot. I made a cup of hot chocolate, without the whipped cream, per Mrs. Greeble's request.

"I was going to come see you today," I said, sitting next to her. I wrapped my hands around my warm mug.

"I'm not surprised. Frankly, I expected a visit sooner. Gossip spreads so quickly in this neighborhood."

Her eyes held a spark of intelligence. She arched a thin white eyebrow at me, telling me quite plainly that she knew I knew.

"You did a good job of keeping your hobby quiet. Mr. Cabrera doesn't know about it, and you know he's the one who spreads the news."

She spared a glance at Brickhouse. "I'm sure he knows now."

"Ach. I didn't tell him. It would hurt his pride if I learned something before him."

Mrs. Greeble smiled weakly and sipped her cocoa.

I pulled my legs onto the chair, tucked them under me. "Do you mind if I ask why?"

"Money, Nina. It's as simple as that. I needed some." She drew in a shaky breath, set her mug on the table. "You may have noticed I'm not in the greatest of health. Bills mount. I should have sold my house long ago. Now it needs many repairs before I can sell, and I need money for the repairs. Winter is coming, my furnace is on the fritz, the windows are single-paned, and my roof leaks."

It was a familiar story in the Mill. Most pensions were pitiful, social security barely enough to pay bills. There was little or nothing for the extras.

"I don't have long to live," she said matter-of-factly.

My breath caught.

Brickhouse put her mug down, leaned in.

"Don't feel sorry for me," Mrs. Greeble said. "I've lived a good life. A long one."

"Do you have children?" Brickhouse asked her.

"Never blessed. There's no one left but me."

My heart hurt for her. I wished I had an iota of her dignity when old and faced with the knowledge that I would die soon.

"My hope with the poker was to raise enough money to move to an assisted living home. Nobody likes to ask for handouts. I really don't want to be a burden to my family."

"But you said—" I began.

Thin lips pulled into a smile. "This neighborhood is my family. Riley, you, Donatelli, Flash, even Maisie, though she's a pain in the ass."

I smiled. She really was.

"To me, a family is made up of people who love and care and nurture each other, it's not always blood that bind people together. Be that as it may, everyone has their own burdens. They don't need mine to add to them."

"You know we don't—"

She held up a bony hand. "It's the way I wanted it. However, it's not the way it's to be. I need to put an end to my 'hobby,' as you call it. I'm too ill to take proper care of things. The dealer I hired has been stealing from me."

"Ach," Brickhouse said.

"And I certainly can't report him." Softly, she said, "It's best to close the doors forever."

"We'll help you with anything you need," I said.

She rose on shaky feet. "No need. I'll be just fine."

Brickhouse and I shared a look. Neither of us believed her for a moment.

I had the sinking feeling that when she said it was "time to close the doors forever," she wasn't just referring to the poker. I needed to buy time so I could think of something, do something . . .

My mother's words echoed suddenly in my head.

It's time for you to learn, perhaps, that sometimes people need to fix themselves.

I shook them out. This wasn't one of those times. It just wasn't. I refused to let it be.

I jumped to my feet. "Well, I hope you'll accept my invitation to our Thanksgiving dinner. There will be plenty of food." *Please, God, let there be plenty of food.* "Plenty of company."

"I don't—"

I pulled my trump card. "It would mean a lot to Riley. I'm sure he'll be well by then."

Her eyes met mine, hers pure steel. "You play dirty, Nina."

"I know."

She smiled. "Thursday. But only because Riley has been such a blessing to me."

Brickhouse offered to escort her home, while I roused Riley for his doctor's appointment.

"Who was at the door?" he asked.

"Mrs. Greeble," I said.

His face paled. I looked at him long and hard. "She's a nice woman."

He blinked. "Yeah. She is."

"I'll meet you downstairs."

In the kitchen, I rinsed the mugs, set them in the dishwasher.

Pulling in a deep breath, I knew what I had to do.

I picked up the phone.

It was time to call in a favor.

I was in line at the pharmacy, picking up a prescription for Riley's strep throat, when Tam called.

"Did you find anything?" I asked her.

"I've got Randall Oh's home phone and address, and also the phone and address of his mother since you mentioned he said he's there a lot. Where better to hide out?"

Smiling, I thought of the conversation I'd had with Perry days earlier. Pulling out my receipt from Kroger the other day, I wrote down the information she found and tucked it into my pocket.

"Thanks, Tam. I owe you."

"Knowing this might help Kit makes me feel better."

I paid the pharmacist and headed for my truck, antibiotics in one hand, cell phone in the other. "Did you hear about the murder of Kent Ingless?" I asked.

"It's been on the news all day. The media coverage made the leap from Kent to Daisy to Kit. It makes me sick. I've been trying to reach Ian about it, but he's not answering."

"There's a lot of that going on today." I told her how I hadn't been able to reach Ana.

"That's strange."

"I know. I'm going to drop Riley off then head over to her place."

"Let me know, or I'll worry." A wail split the air. "Oh, there's Niki up from her nap, gotta go."

I hung up and climbed into my truck. Riley had his head against the window, his eyes closed.

As I turned into the Mill, I caught sight of the fugitive turkey running into the woods. Looked like the SPCA hadn't had any luck in catching the tom.

I drove a little farther down the street and frowned as I pulled up to my house. Unmarked police cars were parked bumper-to-bumper at the curb.

Turning into the drive, I noticed my front door wide open, a swarm of people inside.

This didn't bode well.

I parked behind my mother's car and gently woke Riley. I didn't know what was going on, and decided it might be best if he went over to Bobby's house until I knew what was happening.

He didn't complain, which was a miracle in itself. I watched him cross the road, knock, and go inside without waiting for the door to open.

Ordinarily I'd have been testy about his lack of manners, but right now I had more important things to worry about.

I took the front porch steps two at a time. No one seemed to pay me any notice. I spotted Kevin and Ian speaking with Lewy and Joe and several other men I didn't recognize.

My mother stood in the kitchen, surrounded by empty sacks from Kroger. There wasn't a frozen turkey to be seen. She paused from unpacking when I came in.

"Can you believe the hullabaloo?" she asked.

"Who are they?"

"FBI, DEA? I'm not sure."

I peeked into the living room. "What's going on?"

"Not a clue. They're all very hush-hush. I had to put BeBe outside on her run. She kept jumping on everyone. How's Riley?"

"He's okay. Nasty case of strep throat. He'll be back to his old self in no time."

Pity too, because he'd been kind of lovable lately.

"That's good news. Where is he?"

"At Bobby's. What are you making?"

"Chinese! Dumplings and rice."

I looked at the plethora of ingredients. It was going to be a lot of work. "We could have ordered in."

"Where's the fun in that?"

"Isn't it a little early for dinner?"

"Prep, dear. Dinner will be at seven-thirty sharp."

My mother was a stickler for dinner times.

I left her putting odd-looking ingredients into the fridge. I stood in the doorway of the kitchen, a wide arch that led into the living area. Leaning against the thick framework, I tried to eavesdrop. It wasn't as easy as I would have hoped. Fortunately, Ian spotted me and came over.

"Something's happened," I said. "What? Did you find out what happened to those missing pills?"

"The pills turned up in the storeroom. No one can tell me why they weren't mentioned in the file."

"Then why are you here?"

He dropped his voice. "Ballistics has come in on the bullet pulled out of Daisy."

I was glad I had the arch frame for support. Something about the no-nonsense way he spoke made my knees weak with the imagery. "And?"

"Nina, the bullet came from the same gun that shot Kevin."

I straightened, his words slowly sinking in. I tried to make sense of it. "Whoever shot Kevin also shot Daisy?"

He nodded.

"Why?" I asked.

"I can't say."

"Can't or won't?"

"Can't."

My mother had stopped fussing with dinner and was clearly listening, hanging on every word.

Ian looked over his shoulder and nudged me farther into the kitchen, out of prying eyes.

My head swam, little bits of information clinging together so they didn't drift away.

Kevin had been working for Ian, undercover.

Ian was a DEA agent.

Daisy was suspected of selling drugs.

The link came quickly. "You lied to me! You knew all along Daisy was involved with the Corazón!"

"Come on, Nina. Don't be mad."

"Don't be mad? How can I not? Kit's life is at risk. Kevin was investigating Heavenly Hope while undercover for you when he was shot, wasn't he?"

He didn't say anything.

But his silence said everything.

I put my hands over my face, rubbed my temples. "What was Daisy involved with? Surely not just marijuana and Ecstasy?"

"Daisy was the middleman in a very dangerous drug ring. She supplied the drugs to the street, through Heavenly Hope."

"How was Kent involved?"

"Kent was a chemistry whiz. He made a lot of the stuff Daisy sold."

Aha! So my hunch had been proven right. "Was she really involved with him, personally?"

"According to sources, she fell for him."

I shuddered.

"I know. He wasn't a nice man."

"So, what now?" I asked. "Who killed them?"

"We don't know, Nina. We're still looking for the mastermind of the ring."

"Obviously, Kit's not a suspect anymore."

He didn't say anything.

"Right?" I asked.

Ian dropped his voice. "Let's take this outside," he said.

Nineteen

I followed Ian out the back door. I motioned him to my truck and we both climbed in. The inside was still warm.

I saw my mother watching from the kitchen window.

"Kit can't possibly be a suspect, Ian."

"The police think differently."

"How can they? What does Kit have to do with drugs? Nothing."

"You're wrong about that."

I crossed my arms over my chest. "I don't believe it. Not for a second."

"It's not what you're thinking, Nina."

"Then please explain."

"I know Kit is innocent." He picked at his thumbnail. "What I'm about to tell you could get me fired. Hell, I don't know why I'm telling you at all."

I guessed it had something to do with Tam and wanting to sleep with her again.

"Kit was an informant for me, Nina. Daisy wanted out of the drug system and couldn't do it alone. Kit came to me for help. Kevin was already on the case."

"So Daisy *was* killed because she wanted out?"

"Yes."

"And Kevin was shot . . . why?"

"Honestly, I'm not sure. If it wasn't for ballistics, we might not have tied the two cases together. He was looking into Heavenly Hope but only had one appointment with Daisy when he was shot."

"Maybe she recognized him?"

"No. He was well-disguised."

There had to be a link. Had to.

"Nina, this situation is getting out of control. Someone is running scared, killing off people they feel might incriminate them. You need to stop snooping and stay put. You should be safe here at home with Kevin and Detectives Zalewski and Nickerson watching over you."

Something in his tone made me pay extra attention to the way he'd spoken. "What do you mean, watching over me?"

Looking like he'd been caught red-handed, his chin dropped a notch.

"Oh . . . my . . . God. Kevin didn't come here to recuperate, did he?" I raised my voice when Ian didn't answer. "Did he?"

"No."

"And Lewy and Joe? They weren't following me to find Kit. They were following me to protect me? Bodyguards? Whose idea was that? Wait. Kevin's, right?"

I recalled Kevin's phone call with Ginger. Something about how "she didn't have a clue." The "she" had been me not knowing why he really came to my house.

"We thought it best, Nina. You have a tendency to get into trouble."

"Out! Get out!"

"Nina—"

"Now, Ian."

"Where are you going?"

I found my spare key in the ashtray among pennies and old Tic Tacs and started the truck. "Driving. I need to think."

He climbed out.

"If you hurry, you can get my bodyguards to follow."

I backed out. I knew where I wanted to go. Where I had to go. But there was no way I was going alone. Looking around, I spotted Brickhouse shaking a rug in front of Mr. Cabrera's house, while obviously trying to see what was going on at my place.

I reversed and backed into Mr. Cabrera's driveway. "Get in," I shouted.

Without a second thought, she dropped the rug and waddled as fast as her little legs could carry her brick-shaped self over to the truck. I peeled out just as Lewy and Joe came running out of my house.

I made a series of dizzying turns, lefts and rights through the Mill and connecting neighborhoods, biding my time.

Once I thought I was free from my shadows, I peeled out onto the main road and headed for the highway.

I looked over at Brickhouse. She wore a huge grin on her face. "Ach! This is the most fun I've had since I discovered birth control."

"Too much information!"

She laughed, an evil sounding little chuckle. It broke off suddenly. "This ride isn't going to turn into a scene from *Thelma and Louise,* is it? I know you've never liked me."

"True, but I like me."

I fished the receipt out of my pants pocket. All I remembered was that Randall and his mother lived in Monroe, north of Freedom. "Read that to me, will you?"

Brickhouse clucked. "You eat Chef Boyardee?"

"Other side!"

She rattled off the phone numbers and addresses.

"I don't suppose you have a phone on you?" I asked.

"Evil invention."

I took that as a no.

"We'll just have to do a little drive-by."

"Where are we driving by?"

"Randall Oh's house." I told her the whole sordid truth about Kevin and the ballistics and Joe and Lewy.

For a change she was silent. I let it stretch. I still couldn't believe the news myself. It grated on my last nerve that they'd played me for a fool.

I stopped at a gas station to get directions to Randall's house. A few wrong turns later we happened on his street.

"Do you think this Randall is dangerous?" she asked.

I put the truck in park. "Could be."

"Could I take him?"

"Definitely."

We both went to the door. I knocked and rang the bell, but no one answered.

I peeked in the windows. Darkness covered everything inside. Unless he was hiding out, Randall wasn't home.

"Mama's house next?" Brickhouse asked.

"Yep."

Randall's mother, Ming, lived in an apartment complex near the interstate. We found her place, no problem.

Brickhouse and I waited until someone went into the building and followed them, so we could pounce, unannounced. If Randall was in there, he didn't need any forewarning.

We found Mrs. Oh's apartment and knocked. Apparently the trusting sort, a woman opened the door wide. She took one look at us and closed the door a smidge.

Brickhouse tended to have that effect on people.

"Mrs. Oh?"

"Yes?"

I felt like I was ten years old as I asked, "Is Randall home?"

"Mother?" a voice said from the other room. "Who's there?"

"It's for you," she said in a clipped accent.

"Me?" He came into sight, took one look at me, and cursed a blue streak.

His mother's eyes widened, and Brickhouse clucked. "Respect is so hard to come by, no?"

"A moment of your time?" I asked Randall.

"Who are these women?" his mother asked him, looking suspiciously at us.

"Friends," he said with a fake smile. "Come in, come in. The neighbors will talk."

Mrs. Oh backed up and allowed us to pass. She had slip-covers on her furniture, and the plastic squeaked as we sat down.

"Can we have a minute, Mother?"

She didn't look so sure, but backed out of the room.

"You're tenacious," Randall said to me.

"I've been called worse."

Brickhouse clucked. "By me."

I shot her a look.

Randall laughed, apparently in a jolly mood. "What do you want to know, Nina?"

"I want to find out who killed Daisy."

He laughed. "I love irony."

"What's that supposed to mean?" I asked.

"Daisy hated you, and you're all gung ho to find her killer."

I was sorry Daisy hadn't liked me, but those were her issues, not mine. I refused to let the information bother me. "I'm not really looking for her sake. I'm doing it for Kit." Taking a lesson on gumption from Perry, I said, "Daisy was dealing drugs. Did you know?"

"I took great pains not to know."

"Look, sonny, I don't do well with double-talk," Brick-house said.

He leaned back, the plastic crying in protest. "I had a suspicion. Daisy was very secretive. She didn't want to hire anyone but me. Money flowed in. Her clients seemed to be of questionable origin. Honestly, I didn't want to know. I like what I do. I'm paid well. But, I have morals. That's why I called the cops in the first place. Left an anonymous tip."

"The cops? When?"

He scratched at his goatee. "Two years ago? It was before the questionable clients. I smelled marijuana one day coming from her treatment room. I became suspicious and called. Just to be sure. My reputation is tied to her. To Heavenly Hope."

"What happened with the police?"

"Two officers came out, talked to Daisy, asked to look around a bit. They left soon after. One came back later, looking for treatment, she said."

"She? Do you know her name?"

"I don't recall. I do remember she had beautiful auburn hair, long legs, and a killer body."

Brickhouse and I looked at each other. We only knew of one officer that looked like that.

Ginger.

Twenty

Brickhouse and I made it to the truck before either of us spoke.

Buckling her seat belt, she said, "Holy hell." Perry would have been proud.

"You don't think . . . she can't be . . . involved?" My brain was trying to wrap itself around this information.

"Where is she this week?" Brickhouse asked as I started the truck.

"She flew somewhere to visit her sick mother," I said. "Wyoming, I think."

"Ach. Do we know that for certain?"

We didn't. I'd overheard the call between her and Kevin when she was supposedly still stranded at the airport, but in reality she could have been calling from anywhere.

"And when did she leave?"

"Friday."

"Which simply happens to be the day you find Daisy's body?"

It was a bit of a coincidence.

And not believing in coincidences was one of my top ten commandments.

"Holy hell," I muttered. I turned onto the highway, headed south.

Brickhouse was talking but I wasn't paying attention.

My thoughts whirled. Thoughts about the corruption in the Freedom Police Department, about the timing of Ginger leaving town.

"She's the link," I said aloud. Glancing at Brickhouse, I said, "She's the missing link!"

"If I knew what you were speaking about, perhaps I could be as excited as you."

"No one knew why Kevin was shot," I said. "He'd been in disguise when he went to Heavenly Hope. But what if Ginger had seen him? Being his partner, she would recognize him, incognito or not. They've worked undercover so often she would know immediately."

A cluck so loud came from the seat next to me that I thought for sure Brickhouse had laid an egg. "You think Ginger shot Kevin?"

"And Kent."

"And Kit?"

The ramifications of my theory stacked high in my head. "It makes sense."

"Ach."

I thought aloud. "Let's say Ginger investigates Heavenly Hope two years ago, and discovers Daisy's dealing drugs. She wants a cut. She allows Daisy to keep on dealing, while looking the other way, because she'd be raking in the money. The rest blossoms from there."

"Until Daisy wanted to stop."

"Ginger couldn't let that happen. Maybe for financial reasons, but certainly her career. Her freedom would be at risk if Daisy reached out for help." I wished I could call home, talk to Kevin. He needed to know about this, especially if Ginger never got on that plane. If she'd had a ticket at all.

Brickhouse's icy blue eyes bore into me. "Which she did, asking Kit for help."

More likely, Kit demanded to help. "Who then went to Ian, not knowing Ian was already investigating."

"Using Kevin."

"Right. Ginger must have been shaken when she saw Kevin at Heavenly Hope," I said.

She clucked. "Enough to shoot him. Good thing they're no longer together."

That was an understatement if I ever heard one.

"Why are we getting off here?" Brickhouse asked as I got off the highway one exit early.

"I need a phone, and Ana's place is just around the corner here. It will give me a chance to check on her too, since she hasn't been answering my calls all day."

"Ach, she just might not want to talk to you."

Leave it to Brickhouse to remind me why I didn't like her. I chose to ignore her barb. "Something's wrong."

"You don't think Ginger has gotten to her?"

My stomach dropped. I hadn't thought that at all. "Why would she?"

Brickhouse shrugged, much like Riley. "She knows you're investigating. What better way to distract you?"

My heart in my throat, I stomped on the gas pedal. The truck surged forward.

"Yee-haw!" Brickhouse cried out. "What?" she asked when I gave her the Ceceri Evil Eye.

"This isn't the time to be enjoying yourself."

"Sorry," she mumbled. But as I blew through two yellow lights and cruised through a red, I saw a smile on her face.

The truck hurtled into a parking spot at Ana's condo complex, and lurched forward, then back, as I slammed on the brakes and whipped the gear shift into park.

I ran into the building, Brickhouse huffing and puffing behind me. I made a mental note to give her Duke's number.

I banged on Ana's door. "Ana!"

Brickhouse's normally creamy skin had turned red with exertion. "Did . . . you have to . . . take the stairs . . . so fast?"

"Don't have a heart attack now. I don't have time." I pounded. "Ana!"

"You'd like me . . . to have a heart . . . attack, wouldn't you, Nina . . . Ceceri?" she asked, sounding as though she needed oxygen right away.

"Actually, no." And I meant it. God help me. "Ana!"

"Hold your horses!" I heard her shout from the other side of the door.

Relief swept through me, my heart fluttering back down into my chest.

The door opened. Ana, looking amazing in a simple heather gray sweatsuit, frowned. "It damn well took you long enough."

"What are you talking about?" I asked, my voice rising. "Took me long enough to what?"

"To get here? I would have thought by not answering my phone it would give you a clue that something was wrong. Hello?" Her long dark hair swayed as she jutted her chin. "Didn't I rush home to help you look for Kit? Didn't I? Why wouldn't I answer your call?"

Hands on hips, I said, "I was about to ask you the same thing!"

Brickhouse squeaked out a cluck in between gasps of air.

"Because," Ana said, opening the door wide, "I found him."

Kit sat at her kitchen island, looking like Grizzly Adams. Hair had sprouted on his head, thick and curly, and a straggly beard covered most of his face.

Mine and Brickhouse's mouths dropped open. In perfect unison we muttered, "Holy hell."

Ana dragged us inside and closed the door tight, double-locking it and using the chain.

I kept staring at Kit, thinking I might be hallucinating.

Brickhouse leaned against the door and kept clucking over and over.

No one said anything. The only sound in the room was Brickhouse's soft clucks.

Kit stood.

He'd lost weight. His clothes hung off his tall frame. His body had gone from linebacker to Iron Man. Long and lean yet still strong.

Yet . . .

Alive.

Thank God.

Before I knew it I was running across the room and into his arms. No one gave better hugs than Kit. "You scared the hell out of me!"

"Ach, me too." Brickhouse hip-checked me out of the way. "My turn."

Kit hugged her too, and the tone of her clucks changed from amazed to nurturing. "I like the hair," she said, "but the beard needs to go."

He smiled. "I'll keep that in mind."

I looked at Ana. "You could have called."

"And said what?" she asked. "Hi Nina, I came home from the airport to find Kit in my house. Come on over? Didn't you tell me you thought your phone lines were bugged? I thought it best not to call, and figured your usually nosy self would have checked on me sooner if I didn't answer my phone."

"Hey!" I said. "I was busy! I woke up with Kevin in my bed, had a whole showdown with him, then frozen Cornish game hens mysteriously appeared all throughout the Mill sending Miss Maisie into a tizzy of epic proportions, then Lewy and Joe showed up to tell me Creepy Kent was dead, and then there was this whole thing with Mrs. Greeble and gambling and dying. Then my house was swarmed with DEA and—"

"Ach. Don't forget about Riley's doctor appointment."

"Right. Thank you, Ursula. I also had to take Riley to the doctor. He has strep. He'll be fine. Then I find out that Kevin hasn't really needed recuperation time but only said that so he could keep an eye on me, and that Lewy and Joe were sicced on me by Kevin to be my personal body-guards. And then—then—Ursula and I had to track down

Randall Oh, who told us about a cop who went to investigate Heavenly Hope a few years ago. You know who?" I asked. Without waiting for an answer, I said, "Ginger Ho! Can you even believe it?"

I sat down on the counter stool, inhaled deeply.

"I forgive you," Ana said, batting her eyelashes at me.

I paused for breath, then said, "Oh my God. Kit, are you okay? Were you shot too?"

"The bullet just nicked my arm. I'm fine."

He sat on the stool next to me. Darkness circled his eyes, sadness tugged the fine lines around his mouth and on his forehead into a frown.

I couldn't quite figure out what to say. Or do.

Brickhouse didn't have the same problem. "Ach! What in the hell happened?"

Kit muttered, "What a mess."

Ana took out a bottle of red wine. "Anyone?"

I felt like taking the whole bottle for myself, but had to share with Brickhouse and Ana. Kit declined.

"I dropped Ana off at the airport on Thursday night—" Kit began.

"And then he went to Heavenly Hope," Ana cut in. "He was early, though, because you know how I like to get to the airport three hours before my flight." She set three wineglasses on the counter. We all looked at her, and she gestured with her arms. "Go on," she urged Kit.

I saw the corner of his mouth twitch into a slight grin. "I had made plans with Daisy to help clear out her storeroom. And Ana's right. I was early." He stared into the distance without really seeing anything.

Ana uncorked the wine. "To get rid of the marijuana plants and the rest of the drugs she had hidden. Oh . . . my . . . God. Did you know about the other drugs she sold? Meth and speed and Ecstasy."

"Corazón," I said, "made by none other than Creepy Kent Ingless."

Kit's eyebrows rose. "You've been busy."

"Ach. *We've* been busy." Brickhouse thumped her massive chest.

Ana wasn't impressed. "Anyway," she went on, "Kit and BeBe walk into Heavenly Hope and find Daisy dead."

"I'm sorry," I said to him.

Brickhouse swallowed a huge sip of wine, then clucked. "Me too."

"Next thing he knows, someone is shooting at him. Bullets flying like something out of James Bond."

He looked amused. "Maybe not James Bond."

"Depends," Ana said, "which James."

"Ach, that Daniel Craig is nice eye candy." Brickhouse wriggled her eyebrows.

Ana raised her glass in a toast. "Ursula, I don't agree with you often, but I'll drink to that. Hubba hubba."

"Helloooo," I interrupted.

"Oh!" Ana cried. "Sorry! Anyhoo, Kit escapes. I don't know how. He had to have had a dozen shots fired at him."

"He's a man of steel," Brickhouse said.

Kit looked longingly at my glass of wine. "Do you want a beer?" I asked.

Relief swept through his eyes. I fetched him a can from the fridge.

"Did you see who was shooting you?" Brickhouse asked him.

Ana swirled her wine. "No, he didn't! He was able to run out the back door and almost made it to the woods before one of the bullets nicked his arm."

"What about BeBe?" I asked.

"She wouldn't leave," Kit said softly.

Leave Daisy, I thought. She'd learned loyalty well from her master.

Brickhouse leveled her icy blue gaze on Ana. "Does he speak for himself, Analise Bertoli?"

Kit laughed.

"It's not funny," Ana said. "She's scary when she looks like that."

Kit laughed harder.

Ana stomped. And pouted.

It wasn't pretty.

Okay, it was, because, well, she was Ana. I don't think she could be unattractive if she tried.

I noticed the way Kit looked at her. Warmly.

Ana looked the same way at him.

Interesting.

"He?" I asked. "He said? It was a man who shot you?"

Drawing a finger down his can, Kit left a perfect line in the condensation. "Definitely a man."

"Creepy Kent?" I asked.

Kit shrugged. "May have been. I only met the man once. Daisy always kept us separate."

"Be glad." Brickhouse guzzled the rest of her wine.

"Is he really dead?" Kit asked.

Part of me still couldn't believe it. "Shot point-blank."

"I suppose I'm under suspicion for that too?" he asked.

I hedged. "Ian doesn't think so. The local cops think you're the drug ring leader. They'll come around."

"Yeah. After I get a lethal injection." He scratched at his beard. "I keep playing it over in my head. Walking in, calling for Daisy, finding her in the storeroom. I kept thinking of how ironic it was."

"What?" I asked.

"That she had wanted out of selling illegal drugs because she didn't want to be responsible for anyone overdosing. She didn't want to cause someone else's death. And it turns out those drugs are what killed her. To top it off, she was killed surrounded by the stuff. It almost felt like fate was mocking her." He shook his head. "What a waste."

Surrounded by? "The room was just about empty when I found her."

"I know," he said. "Whoever killed her must have gone for boxes. That's when I showed up, found Daisy."

Ana broke in. "Kit never heard anyone come back,

though. Neither did BeBe. He just saw the boxes on the floor when he ran out."

"We were both in shock, I guess," Kit said. "I was able to get away, but BeBe stayed with Daisy. Is she okay? The news reports never mentioned her."

"BeBe's just fine. She misses you, but is still drooling up a storm. She's scared of turkeys, though. You might want to work on that."

He arched an eyebrow in question.

"Don't ask," I said. "Did the shooter follow you into the woods?"

Kit shook his head.

Ana set her glass on the counter. "Kit hid in the woods until he thought it was safe—he'd seen a car drive away—then he ran to his truck."

That explained the bloodstains.

"But I didn't have my keys," he said. "I must have dropped them in Heavenly Hope."

"Actually," I interrupted, "you lost them in the woods. The police found them."

He nodded. "I sat in my truck a long time, and finally decided I had to call the police. My cell had died by that time, but I'd seen a dark car pull out of the driveway about an hour before that so I thought it was safe to go back inside."

Ana tossed her hair over her shoulder. "So he was headed back inside to call 911, and to get BeBe, when a silhouette appeared in Heavenly Hope's doorway—" She stomped her foot again. "Don't look at me like that, Ursula!"

Brickhouse clucked. "Let the man tell his own story!"

If Ana didn't keep her mouth shut, I wouldn't put it past Brickhouse to bean her on the head with the wine bottle.

Kit picked up the story. "Ana's right. A silhouette appeared in the doorway. I thought I was a goner."

"Was it a woman?" I asked, still hoping to tie Ginger into this somehow.

"No," Ana said.

With another warning look from Brickhouse, Ana muttered, "Sorry. You tell it, Kit."

"It was a man. Medium build, medium height. I couldn't see much more."

"Did he say anything to you?" Brickhouse asked, going for seconds on the wine.

Ana couldn't control herself. Excitedly, she lowered her voice and imitated a man, saying, "'Run. Because no one will ever believe you.'"

I didn't have time to react when Brickhouse lunged at her, spewing curses in German.

Twenty-One

"Ach. Maybe Ginger had hooked up with Creepy Kent?"

I couldn't see it. I wanted to think that Ginger had better taste in men.

Although she had picked Kevin.

Then again, so had I.

But did she shoot him?

Lord knows there'd been days I wanted to.

Brickhouse and I were on our way home, and we were discussing whether Ginger was involved with Daisy's death. It had taken Kit's strength to pull Brickhouse off Ana back at the condo. Not much damage had been done. Just a little squishing. "You didn't have to attack Ana, you know."

"I warned her."

Fair enough—she had.

I'd decided not to call Kevin.

Honestly, I had nothing to say. There was no way on God's green earth I'd tell him where Kit was hiding. I wish I could tell him I knew who'd shot Daisy. And who'd shot him. But I didn't know.

And an evil part of me wished I could say it was Ginger.

For karma's sake.

Unfortunately, I couldn't find any evidence that she'd been mixed up in Daisy's death at all.

"Kent was definitely involved," I said.

Brickhouse clucked. "I've always suspected you weren't the sharpest knife in the drawer, but that statement would confirm it, Nina Ceceri, since we've established that Kent was involved up to the tips of his silver hair."

"You sound like Perry," I said, missing him. I hoped he was feeling better.

"Ach. Are you trying to change the subject?"

"Not at all. I'm always up for a discussion of my mental acuity."

She smiled. It was a rare sighting.

"I was simply talking aloud," I explained, "trying to get facts straight in my head."

"Seems simple to me. Kent was the ringleader. He shot Kevin because he must have suspected he was undercover, and he shot Daisy because she wanted out of the business but knew too much."

Talk about not the sharpest knife. However, I valued my life, so I simply said, "And who shot Kent?"

She grumbled when she couldn't come up with an answer.

"You know," I said, "Randall Oh is of medium build, medium height."

Clucking, she grumbled, "He didn't seem the type to lie. I can usually tell."

"Sociopaths lie very well."

"Ach."

"It makes sense. He had just as much access to the drugs as Daisy. Let's say they were both selling drugs. Only she wants out, wants to make Heavenly Hope legit. What does that do to Randall?"

"Cuts his income."

"Sounds like motive to me. So, he kills Daisy, knowing she was going to meet with Kit that night. Maybe he'd been planning on killing Kit too, making it look like a murder-suicide. But Kit is early. Shows up before Randall can clear out the inventory, because the last thing he wants is for the police to confiscate his goods."

"I can see it," Brickhouse said.

"Plus, Randall probably saw Kent talking to me at the viewing yesterday and became worried that Kent was telling secrets in his state of grief. Is it a coincidence that Kent is dead the next day? You know how I feel about coincidences. Who had the most to lose if Daisy strayed onto the straight and narrow path? Kent for certain. And Randall if he'd had anything to do with the drugs. The more I think about it, the more sure I become that he had a lot to do with the drugs."

"I liked Randall's mother too. Poor thing is going to be devastated."

The more I thought about Randall being behind the murders, the more I liked the idea.

It made sense when nothing else did.

I was all for making sense for a change.

My inner voice seconded that notion.

Besides, I was fresh out of suspects.

My headlights swept across Mrs. Daasch's house as I turned the corner onto my street. I half expected Bobby to be out fixing the gutters, but all the lights were off.

I parked in my driveway behind Ian's car, cut my lights. Lewy and Joe's car was half on the curb, half on the street. I smiled. They weren't going to be happy I lost them.

"Okay," I said. "Not a word about Kit."

"Duh," she said.

It made me laugh because it was so unlike her and so much like something Riley would say. "Too much time with Riley?" I asked.

"I suppose so."

"I'd like to get Ian alone if I can. Tell him most of what I know. I think we can trust him."

"I'll distract the others," she said.

I didn't want to know how. "Sounds like a plan. You ready?"

"Ja."

Aha! I knew that was German for yes. It was just about the only word in German I knew, besides "schnitzel."

I looked at her. "Is it wrong that I wanted Ginger involved?"

"Ach. Yes." She opened the door, slid out.

Great.

The loud sounds of *gobble gobble gobble* echoed down the street. I hoped the turkey wasn't in futile search of its mate.

As I climbed the front steps I made a mental note to find a second to call Maddie to let her know about Kit. I opened the front door to wonderful smells. The scent of Chinese spices made my stomach rumble. I heard sizzling coming from the kitchen.

Kevin, Ian, Lewy, and Joe glared at us. Amazingly, it didn't ruin my appetite.

"Where have you been?" Kevin asked.

"Driving." I still wasn't happy with him. One thing was certain—he wouldn't be sleeping there tonight. "Why? Did anything happen while I was gone?"

"Did it?" Kevin asked.

"I'm here. In one piece. It's a miracle. Ursula?"

"One piece," she said, patting herself down.

"*Chérie*! You're home! Just in time to help me with dinner. Oh! Ursula, Donatelli is looking for you. He was out chasing the fugitive turkey when the turkey attacked him. He's fine, scratched a bit, but just fine. I think he wants you to tend to him. Refused my offer," she said, sounding a bit put out.

Brickhouse didn't spare a glance in my direction. She bid her good-byes and waddled to the door.

So much for distraction.

Once she left, my mother dragged me into the kitchen. "Are you okay, *chérie*?"

It took me a second to realize she was talking about what happened with Ian and his revelations about Kevin. The men must have been talking while I was gone.

"I'm all right. Dinner smells good." She was sautéing onions and it smelled heavenly. Vegetables covered the countertop, and rice simmered on the stovetop.

"You can help me slice."

Ian was fully focused on the conversation he was having. I really could have used Brickhouse's help.

I picked up a paring knife and sliced some mushrooms, though I despised them. "Did Riley make it back okay?"

"He's upstairs sleeping. BeBe is keeping him company."

"Did he eat anything?"

"Not much."

"The doctor said he wouldn't for a day or two. Personally, I think he's scared we're going to give him more pea soup."

"He has reason to fear the soup." My mother grinned. "It's terrible."

Ha! I knew it.

I finished with the mushrooms, set down my knife. "I'm going to check on Ry."

I tried to catch Ian's eye, but he wouldn't look at me. I couldn't say I blamed him after I kicked him out of my truck earlier, but really. How scary would facing me be?

Apparently, a lot. Not one of the men looked my way as I headed for the stairs.

BeBe must have heard me coming. She was waiting when I pushed open Riley's door, her tail thumping, drool oozing.

Darkness had long since fallen, and Riley's room was pitch-black. I reached for the overhead switch, then stopped myself. I didn't want to wake him with a flood of artificial light.

Leaning over his desk, I followed the cord of the lava lamp until I found the switch. I ran my finger over the dial, heard the clicking, but the lamp didn't flutter to life.

I backtracked into the hall, BeBe at my feet, and turned on the light. It filtered into Riley's room, allowing me to make out shapes and shadows.

Creeping to the bed, I felt Riley's head. Still warm.

A tray with a bottle of water and some crackers sat on his desk. I moved the water to his nightstand and realized it was too dark for him to see it there if he needed it.

I tried the switch on the lava lamp again. Still didn't work. Was it plugged in? Fumbling in the darkness, I started at the base of the lamp to follow the cord of the socket. BeBe nudged me from behind and knocked me forward into the lamp. I grabbed the base not realizing the top wasn't attached. The lava globe hit the carpet with a loud thump.

Once I righted myself, I noticed the base wasn't empty.

I reached inside.

The noise from the commotion must have awoken Riley, because he sat up just in time to see me pull out a wad of papers.

He came fully awake rather quickly. "You don't need to see those!" he said, lunging.

I pulled my hand away. He tumbled to the floor. BeBe thought it was a game and plopped down and started rolling on top of Riley.

"Get her off me!" he said.

She licked and slobbered.

I smiled and declined to help him. There went my Stepmother of the Year award again. Maybe I just wasn't cut out for it.

I backed toward his doorway and flipped on the overhead light.

"My eyes! My eyes!" Riley said.

"Close them," I advised unsympathetically, unfolding the papers.

I'd been expecting to find money or something related to his poker playing. Instead I found receipts. Three of them.

My eyes widened with each one.

Riley finally managed to dislodge BeBe and hauled himself back into bed. He glowered at me.

He was good at it. But not good enough.

"Want to explain?" I asked.

"Not really."

I sat down on the edge of the desk. BeBe looked between Riley and me and chose to jump on the bed. She circled three times and dropped. Riley tugged his leg out from under her.

"Do you know how much grief you've caused everyone?"

Splotches covered his neck, crept up his face. Since he was a kid, it had been his default reaction to being overly upset. Hives. He'd be an itchy mess in no time.

"I was trying to help!" Throwing himself back against his pillows, he folded his arms over his chest. His chin thrust out stubbornly.

I took a second to absorb what he was saying while I looked at the receipts for two turkeys, one rooster, and twenty Cornish game hens.

Then I remembered what he'd told me.

Kit told me that sometimes it's important to help people even when they don't want the help.

And what Mrs. Greeble had said.

Nobody likes to ask for handouts. I really don't want to be a burden to my family.

"I see," I finally said to Riley.

"You do?" His eyes looked cautious.

"I really do." I smiled. "It was sweet of you. The thought, at least."

"I didn't know the turkeys were alive!"

I bit back a laugh. That probably wouldn't go over too well with his teenage pride.

"I had been wondering why they were so expensive."

I checked the receipt. Holy smokes!

"I tried tying them up, but they escaped."

I almost laughed again at the image of Riley wrangling

two turkeys and trying to tether them. "And the rooster?" I squeaked out.

"Well, I didn't want to do turkeys again, so I thought chicken would be close enough, but I only bought one, just in case it was alive too."

"Good thinking," I mumbled.

"But then it showed up alive, and as a rooster, and I couldn't catch him once I got him out of the box."

I chuckled. I couldn't help it.

"It's not funny!" But I noticed his lip curling up into a smile.

"I know, I know," I said, laughing a little bit harder. "And the hens?"

He threw his hands in the air. "I finally figured out to buy frozen ones. I couldn't afford frozen turkeys anymore, so I had to get the hens, and now no one will eat them!"

I couldn't help it. I let the laughter loose.

BeBe cocked her head.

It only took Riley a minute to join me. Tears streamed and I couldn't catch my breath.

My mother stuck her head in the door. "What on earth?" she said.

It only made Riley and me laugh harder.

When she realized we weren't going to answer, she huffed and went back downstairs.

My stomach hurt from laughing so hard. "No . . . wonder you . . . were . . . saying . . . gobble, gobble . . . in your sleep!"

"I did not!"

I nodded, laughed, and gasped for breath all at the same time. "Did."

It took a good minute to pull myself together, but I still found myself chuckling whenever I looked at the receipts. I tucked them back into the base of the lava lamp and replaced the globe. The lamp had been unplugged, after all. Nice to know Riley had the good sense not to create a fire hazard.

"What are you going to do?" he asked.

"About what?"

"The turkeys?"

"What turkeys?" I smiled.

He smiled too. It bloomed across his whole splotchy face.

"Look," I said, "what you did was a wonderful gesture. I'm actually proud of you. You went about it all the wrong way, but we learn from our mistakes. I think with the state Miss Maisie is in, we'll keep this between us."

He nodded.

"But Ry, gambling is never a good way to earn money. In the end you'll lose much more than you'll ever gain. And not just money."

His shoulders squared. "I don't gamble for money. Well, not much money."

My eyebrows rose. "Then how did you pay for the turkeys?"

"I worked! Hard. Mrs. Greeble's house is falling apart!"

I tried to process what he was saying. "You didn't gamble at her house?"

"I'd like to say I didn't try, but she wouldn't let me. Told me I was too young."

Thank you, Mrs. Greeble.

"Well, she's right."

"Whatever. I can't wait till I'm older."

I almost laughed again. He didn't have a clue what was in store for him. But that was for him to learn, over time. "How about we master driving first?"

He settled down into his bed. "Deal."

I walked over to the door and said, "You coming, BeBe?"

She lifted her head, put it back down.

Traitor.

"If you're hungry, come on down. Grandma Cel is making Chinese."

"Almost as bad as the split pea soup."

"Clearly that fever is affecting your brain cells."

"Gobble, gobble."

Twenty-Two

"Look," my mother said, raising the shade and motioning out the window.

I fully expected to see Miss Maisie picketing poultry products. Instead I saw Mario's crunched Saturn sitting at the curb behind Lewy and Joe's unmarked car.

"What's that doing here?"

"Apparently, Perry gave the tow truck driver your address." She lowered the shade. "The driver was kind enough to apologize for the delay. He's been backlogged because of the snow."

"Great. We can't let Mario see it. Perry's life will be at risk."

"Pah. Not to worry. I know someone."

"Do I want to know?"

"No, *chérie*. No."

I took her word for it.

"Make yourself useful. Chop chop." My mother stood at the counter, cutting dough into rectangles for the dumplings. "First the carrots, then the scallions."

Lewy wandered into the kitchen as I hacked off the business end of the carrot. He took a step back. "Should I be scared?"

"Yes."

"Are you still mad?" he asked me.

"Yes."

"It was for your own good."

My mother arched an eyebrow, and I tightened my grip on the knife. "You may want to rethink that conclusion," I said, chopping away.

"Too big," my mother chastised. "Dice, *chérie*, dice."

Thank goodness there were only two carrots.

Lewy leaned on the counter. "We were worried," he said.

I released my grip just a bit as I diced like a pro. "That's better."

"Why worry?" my mother asked. "We know Kit is innocent."

"Actually we don't know that," Lewy said, "and honestly, we were more worried Nina would get herself into trouble."

My mother laughed.

So did Lewy.

I didn't see what was so amusing. And said so. Which made them laugh harder.

Hmmph.

I finished with the carrots and grabbed the bunch of scallions. "All of it, *chérie*. White part too."

"The root too?" I asked innocently.

"No one likes a smartass, *chérie*."

Lewy grabbed a stalk of celery to nibble on, and my mother slapped his hand and took back the celery. "Dinner will be soon enough."

"What's this?" I asked, turning over a thick, light brown, nubby something that looked like it had just been pulled out of the ground.

"That's—"

Raising quite the ruckus, BeBe trotted downstairs. How she didn't slide right down, I don't know. She raced into the kitchen, checked her empty food bowl, slurped some water, and nearly knocked Lewy over with her thrashing tail.

"What?" I asked, ignoring BeBe's shenanigans.

"Ginger root," my mother said, stirring the onions and taking them off the heat.

BeBe pranced to the laundry room, which opened into the side yard. Her tail wagged, drool pooled.

"Looks like she needs to go out," my mother said, looking at me.

I looked at Lewy.

He said, "Don't look at me. I love dogs, but not that much."

"Fine." I slid off my stool. "I thought ginger came in a can?"

My mother dramatically put her forearm to her head. "I have failed as a mother."

BeBe detoured for more water.

"You can buy ground ginger in a can, *chérie*, but I prefer to grate my own," my mother said. She handed Lewy a grater. "Make yourself useful."

Wise as he was, he didn't argue. He held out his hand to me.

"But it looks so . . . " I held the root up, turned it over in my palm.

"Gnarly?"

"No, it looks like . . . "

They waited.

"I don't know. It looks familiar."

BeBe whimpered.

"All right, all right. Come on." I pulled on a coat, slipped on my Keds.

I opened the back door and BeBe shot out, dashing into the night.

In the distance I heard the turkey gobbling, a throaty, warbly sound I found soothing. He was free. He was safe.

BeBe pranced and sniffed, in no hurry to do her business.

I sat on the step of Mr. Cabrera's gazebo, picked up a branch. In the mulch bed, I traced the shape of the ginger root, hoping it would trigger what it reminded me of.

In my doodling I drew a circle around it, and nearly jumped clear out of my skin.

Oh . . . my . . . God.

The ginger root looked exactly like a heart. A real heart. It reminded me of the image I'd seen on the Corazón.

Ginger root looked like a heart.

Coincidence?

I didn't think so. Ginger Barlow had to be involved with the Ecstasy.

I jumped up. "BeBe! Come!"

I ran toward the house. The back door opened and BeBe ran inside. Lewy came out, his face lit. "Nina!"

"What?"

"The station just called. Kit's turned himself in."

"What?" He hadn't said a word about turning himself in. "Really?"

"He's asking for you, wants to make sure you call a lawyer for him."

My mind flew. Lawyers, lawyers . . .

"Josh! Bobby's cousin." He was slime, but he'd do in a pinch. I glanced across the street. "Let me just run over and ask Bobby to get in touch with him."

"Call him from the road. Come on. I'll drive." He ran to the Ford, opened my door, then dashed around to his side.

I hurried to keep up. Mario's car looked so sad in comparison to the shiny Taurus.

Then I remembered. Ginger! "Wait," I said. "I just need a minute. I've got to talk to Ian."

"We don't have time, Nina! Kit's waiting for you."

He was right. Ian could wait. Yet . . . "It really will take a second." I don't know why I was being so stubborn. Perhaps I just wanted to see Kevin's face when he heard the news about Ginger.

Which was really awful of me.

So awful, I couldn't bring myself to do it.

I turned to get in the car when I saw Lewy pointing a gun at me.

I blinked, not sure I believed what I was seeing. "Get in the car, Nina."

Oh no. Uh-uh. Nothing good would come of me getting in that car. "What are you doing, Lewy?"

"You couldn't just mind your own business, could you?"

Was there a good answer to that question?

"I don't understand," I said. And I didn't. What did Lewy have to do with anything that was going on?

Then a little nugget of information tumbled to the forefront of my consciousness. Lewy had once been Ginger's partner.

About the time Heavenly Hope had been investigated by Ginger and her partner . . .

"Get in the car," he ordered.

"No."

I glanced toward the house. The shades were drawn. Across the street, Bobby's blinds were closed tight. Even Mr. Cabrera had his drapes shut.

Just my luck.

"Get . . . in . . . the . . . car."

I took a step back. Had he shot Kevin? Daisy? Kit? Kent? Was he a cold-blooded killer? "No."

"I will shoot you."

"Like you shot Kevin? Daisy? Kit? Kent?"

His eyes narrowed. "Another difference between you and Leah. She was smart enough to know when to keep her mouth shut."

"Yeah, well, I'm not Leah." I struggled to buy time. "Who pulled the strings, Lewy? You or Ginger?"

He raised his gun, took aim at me. "Last chance."

What to do? What to do? I could think of only one thing.

I screamed.

Out of nowhere wings flapped and feathers flew as the big fugitive turkey swooped in. Claws extended, it attacked.

Everything happened in a blur. Shouting voices, more screams, gobbling, blood, gunshots. Somehow I ended up behind Mario's car. Above my head, car windows shattered. Glass rained down on my hair, skittered down my arms and onto the street.

I covered my head, tucked my chin, and—of all things—hoped the stupid turkey was okay.

Blood dripped into my eyes, and it had to be my own, but I didn't feel any pain. Before I knew it, I was being lifted up. I fought for a second before Bobby's voice reached in and pulled me out of my fear.

He cupped my head, keeping it close to his chest. Through his T-shirt his racing heart pounded my cheek.

"Is she okay?" I heard my mother ask.

Bobby pulled back and looked at me. "Maybe a few stitches. She'll be all right."

"Stitches?"

"Looks like the turkey sliced your forehead."

My mother held my face in one hand while she dabbed at my forehead with a handkerchief. "Amazing. It looks like a perfect little heart."

I closed my eyes. As if I'd need any permanent reminders about this night.

Sirens wailed in the distance.

"Where's Lewy?" I asked.

"On the other side of the car," Bobby said.

"Is he dead?"

My mother laughed. "He wishes. By the time the turkey, Bobby, Kevin, Ian, Joe, and Riley jumped him, he was the little squished piggy at the bottom of the pile."

I looked over my shoulder. Riley stood with Kevin, side by side, watching me. It had never been clearer how much they needed each other.

Especially now.

"You want to go over?" Bobby asked.

I looked up at him. "I'm right where I need to be."

He kissed the top of my head.

Three police cars swerved to a stop. Uniformed officers swarmed.

"I better get some coffee on," my mother said. She kissed my cheeks, then hurried into the house.

Bobby walked me over to his front steps. "How's the turkey?" I asked.

"Gone," he said. "It flew off."

"I hope it's okay."

"I'm sure it is." Obviously trying to lighten the mood, he said, "I don't suppose you want to call off Thanksgiving?"

"You're not getting out of it that easy, Bobby Mac-Kenna."

"A guy can try, right?"

Across the street Ian yanked Lewy to his feet. Handcuffs bound his wrists. Blood covered his face. I wondered if it was a result of the wild turkey or of the men trying to protect me.

Not that it mattered.

Ian pushed Lewy past Mario's shot-up car, toward a cruiser.

I curled closer into the nook of Bobby's arm. "Besides, don't you think we have a lot to be thankful for this year?"

"Yeah, I do."

"Although . . ."

"What?"

"Mario's going to pitch a fit when he sees his car."

Twenty-Three

"What did you think of Lowther House?" I asked Mrs. Greeble as I drove toward home. Thanksgiving morning had dawned sunny and warm, all traces of snow long gone.

"It was wonderful, Nina. I still don't understand how you were able to get me in."

"As I told you, Pippi owed me a favor."

"Must have been quite some favor."

"It was."

I couldn't have been happier that Pippi had agreed to let Mrs. Greeble become a resident of Lowther House for the rest of her days, paying only what she could.

"Why, Nina?"

"Why?"

"Why help me?"

"Simple," I said, pulling into my driveway. "Because I can."

When I came to a stop, her hand shook as she placed it on mine. "Thank you."

"You're welcome."

I helped her into the house, settled her on the sofa next to my father, shook him awake so he'd have to be social, and went into the kitchen to see if my mother had everything under control.

Kit had slept there last night but he'd gone out earlier with BeBe. He didn't say where. I didn't ask.

The delicious scents of garlic and tomato sauce filled the air.

"Four lasagnas should be enough, correct, *chérie*?"

"More than. Thank you so much for cooking, Mom. No one makes better lasagna than you."

She pinched my cheek. "What are mamas for? How did the visit go?"

"Very well. Mrs. Greeble moves into Lowther House tomorrow."

"You did a good thing."

"It feels good. A bit like extortion, but good."

"All's well that ends well, no?"

"I suppose. Is Riley upstairs?"

"With Kevin."

I headed that way. I knew I should have kicked Kevin out Tuesday night, but after everything that happened, it didn't seem so urgent. He was packed and ready to leave after dinner, and he was hoping Riley would go with him.

Kevin had come to me yesterday with the news. As much as I hated to lose Riley, he belonged with his dad. Being together was truly the bond that would help both of them heal.

I was going to miss him like crazy.

Thankfully, Kevin agreed to let Riley stay here on weekends, and starting this summer, Ry was going to work for me as Kit's apprentice.

The job wouldn't be easy, but it would teach him the value of hard work, responsibility, and hopefully keep him out of trouble.

I wasn't holding my breath.

At the top of the stairs, I knocked on Riley's ajar door and poked my head in. He and Kevin sat on the bed. Neither said hello.

"He wants to stay until Sunday," Kevin said.

"Good. I'll need a few days to get used to the idea of his leaving."

Kevin rose. "And it will give me time to move out of Ginger's place and into one of my own."

Ginger. None of us had talked about her. Of how Lewy had tricked her into becoming part of his drug ring, of how she had no way out, of how he used a ginger root as the Ecstasy design to remind her of her involvement, to ensure her silence. Terrified for her own life, she'd run when she witnessed Lewy kill Daisy and was now safe and sound in Wyoming with her mother. Where she planned to stay. Word was, she agreed to testify against Lewy for her freedom, but would never work in law enforcement again.

The Freedom PD was taking quite a hit, but weathering well. They'd found Daisy's hard drive and a list of her clients, which included one Dr. Marvin Partridge. Brickhouse had been right about her former student.

Turned out Randall Oh had been telling Brickhouse and me the truth, and I felt badly for thinking he was a cold-blooded murderer.

Not enough to call him and apologize, mind you.

All charges against Kit had been dropped, and Joe was reassigned a new partner.

"Anyone here?" Kevin asked.

"Mrs. Greeble, my dad, my mom."

"You sure you don't mind me staying for dinner?"

"I'm sure. No complaining about lasagna, though."

Even if there'd been a turkey left on the store shelf, I wouldn't have bought it. I didn't think I'd ever be able to eat it again, not after one saved my life.

"Do we at least have stuffing?" he said.

"Yeah, it's called ricotta cheese."

He grumbled his way past me, out the door.

My cell phone rang, and I checked the caller ID. "Thanks for calling me back, Claudia," I said. I wouldn't have answered if it had been anyone else.

Brickhouse's daughter sounded confused. "Is something wrong, Nina?"

"Not at all." I smiled at Riley, who was clearly eavesdropping. I asked her about ever having duped Brickhouse. "Between you and me," I added.

She laughed. "All the time, Nina. And between you and me? I'm due to be married soon. But the truth is, I eloped almost a year ago. My mother doesn't have a clue."

Vindication never felt so good!

I offered congratulations and hung up, feeling proud of myself.

"What was that all about?" Riley asked.

"Can't tell. So," I said, sitting on the bed, "are you going to miss me?"

His lips had returned to a soft pink. His fever had broken yesterday and he was feeling normal again. "No."

Definitely normal again.

"Oh. Well." I elbowed his ribs. "I'm not going to miss you either."

"Good we got that straight."

"Definitely," I said.

"Did you see Bobby's column?" I asked, standing.

"Yeah. It was okay."

I laughed. "Don't gush. It doesn't become you."

Bobby had written a touching column about the turkey that saved me, and about how it had been given a home on a farm north of the city where it was guaranteed to never become someone's dinner.

Ian had graciously taken the turkey in, and Tam insisted he adopt the turkey captured the other day and Gregory Peck as well.

Ian hadn't complained a bit. Penance, I suppose, for tricking me.

I loved that Tam.

"Did you give Booby an answer yet?"

I gave him the Ceceri Evil Eye until he corrected himself.

"Fine, Bobby. Did you give him an answer yet?"

The incident with Lewy the other night had finally propelled me to tell Bobby how I felt about him. And him about me. He proposed that night while I was being stitched up in the hospital, which was more romantic than one would think.

I hadn't given him an answer yet.

With more than a bit of derision, Riley said, "You know, you need to take into consideration that he's not going to make any money writing. How's he going to pay his bills? How's he going to be able to keep you supplied with cookie dough?"

Ah. He was worried. How sweet. Not that I said so. I could only imagine the attitude shift that would cause.

"But you love him, right? And he loves you?"

"Yeah, but life is a little more complicated than that."

He turned toward me, his blue eyes serious. "No it's not."

Maybe, just maybe, he was right.

I hated when that happened.

I didn't dare reach out and tousle his hair, though I wanted to. "Mrs. Greeble's downstairs. I'm sure she wants to tell you all about Lowther House."

"I'll be down after I shower," he said, turning up his stereo, dismissing me.

I couldn't believe I was going to miss the little bugger.

But I was. I closed his door behind me and nearly jumped clear out of my fuzzy socks when I saw Kevin standing there.

Arms crossed, chin down, he didn't look happy. "I owe you an apology," he said. "For the other day."

Eyebrow raised, I asked, "Which part?"

He rolled his eyes. "For all of it, I suppose. But mostly the other morning. You were right, about Leah."

Riley's door thumped from a song with heavy bass.

"I know."

He cracked a smile. "I've got a lot of mental stuff to

work through. Thanks for not putting up a fuss about Riley coming to live with me."

"You're welcome. It's not going to be easy to let him go. He's grown on me. A bit like lichen to a shady rock."

Bushy eyebrows dipped quizzically.

"Never mind," I said. "I'll miss him."

Fidgeting, Kevin wouldn't look at me. His Adam's apple bobbed. Finally, he met my eyes. "You couldn't have been a better mom to him. I mean it, Nina."

Tears sprang immediately. I fought to keep them from spilling over. "Thank you for letting me be his mom."

"You always will be." He nodded, turned, and hurried down the stairs.

Riley's door flew open and he nearly knocked me over. I hadn't even noticed the stereo going off.

He looked at me like I was nuts. "What are you doing?" he asked.

"What?"

"Standing there?"

"Um, uh—"

"Whatever," he said, brushing past me and into the bathroom.

I smiled and went downstairs. Brickhouse and Mr. Cabrera had shown up. Bobby too. My mother had him slicing cucumbers. He glanced up at me with a "Help me" look in his eye.

Flash and Miss Maisie had joined Mrs. Greeble, Kevin, and my dad in the living room, and just as I was about to rescue Bobby, the doorbell rang.

I opened it. BeBe rushed in, tail thrashing, drool oozing. On the stoop, Kit and Ana held hands.

Very interesting.

Ana saw me looking, and her eyes dared me to say something.

Nope. Uh-uh. Just call me Nina Colette Ceceri I'm So Happy for Them, Please Don't Let Them Screw It Up Quinn.

Mac, Bobby's grandfather, was just climbing the stairs as Ana and Kit passed through the door. He gave me a big kiss on my lips and said, "I promise not to steal anything."

"That's good to hear, Mac."

I relieved Bobby from the cucumbers just as Ian, Tam, and Niki showed up. Not long afterward, Mario and Perry arrived. My mother, true to her word, had contacted someone who took Mario's car away and promised to return it good as new, well . . . used, in two weeks. Much to Mario's relief.

And Perry's dismay. He'd been hoping the car was gone for good.

Riley came down the stairs, and I couldn't help but notice how Mrs. Greeble's face lit up. He dutifully kissed her cheek and let her ruffle his hair.

Josh, Bobby's sleazy cousin, arrived next. To my surprise, he brought a nice bottle of wine. And Bobby had been worried about his family. It gave me hope.

Jean-Claude, Shay, Marty, and Jeff came as a group. They hadn't had other plans, and really, what were a few more people? It was great to see their faces when they spotted Kit.

My sister Maria had called to say she was going to be late and not to keep dinner. She had to suffer through an earlier dinner at her in-laws.

"Dinner is ready," my mother called out. BeBe barked happily.

We'd decided to serve the meal buffet-style, since there was no way we'd fit everyone around my kitchen table.

I found a quiet corner, waiting until everyone else was done dishing up lasagna, garlic bread, salad, and antipasto.

"You have the strangest look on your face," Bobby said, walking over to me.

"I'm thinking."

"About?"

I motioned with my head to all the people trying to

squeeze into my kitchen. "Mrs. Greeble is right. Blood isn't always the tie that binds. Families are made up of people who love and care and nurture each other. I guess I'm thankful for my family. The whole kit and caboodle."

He put his arm around me and pulled me close. "Me too."

"Speaking of, where's the rest of your family?"

"My family?" he asked, looking innocent.

"Yes, your family."

A mischievous light entered his eyes. "I might have forgotten to invite them."

Smiling, I said, "You're in so much trouble."

"How much?"

"Lots." I looked into his eyes. "Your family, Bobby?"

"Yeah?"

"Just be sure they're at our wedding."

From the Desk of Nina Quinn

Heading into December is the best time to prepare your gardening tools for their long winter's nap. In doing so, you will be ready to hit the soil immediately upon sighting the earliest crocus come springtime.

First things first. Gather together all your tools and take stock. What needs to be replaced? What needs repair? What needs to be given a good scrubbing? Sort your tools into piles, roll up your sleeves, and dig in.

Where's Mr. Clean When You Need Him?

It's important to clean your tools before putting them away for the winter. Use a wire brush or steel wool to remove dirt and other garden debris. Get rid of pesky rust spots by using steel wool or a fine grit sandpaper.

Can I Get a Pedicure with That?

To sharpen the edges on your tools, use a heavy-duty steel file, making sure to file in one direction only. Follow up with a whetstone to smooth your edges to a razor-fine finish.

Use heavy grit sandpaper on wooden handles to smooth out rough edges. Nobody wants springtime splinters.

No Trans-Fats Allowed

Use linseed oil, or a mixture of half linseed/half mineral oil, to keep your wooden handles in good shape. The oil will protect the handles from absorbing moisture and cracking. After the oil dries, use your creativity to paint your handles in bright colors. It's fun, and it will be easy to spot your tools in the garden.

If your tools have fiberglass handles, you can use a bit of wax to keep them smooth.

For your metal tools, be sure to spray lubricant oil to keep all parts in proper working order and to keep rust from forming.

Do You Take Credit?

If you find your favorite trowel is beyond repair, winter is the perfect time of year to shop for new tools. Why? Off-season sales! Take advantage and stock up. You'll be ready for spring in no time at all.

Best wishes for happy gardening!

Investigate the Hottest New Mysteries!

Sign up for the FREE HarperCollins monthly mystery newsletter,

The Scene of the Crime,

and get to know your favorite authors, win free books, and be the first to learn about the best new mysteries going on sale.

To register, simply go to www.HarperCollins.com, visit our mystery channel page, and at the bottom of the page, enter your email address where it states "Sign up for our mystery newsletter." Then you can tap into monthly Hot Reads, check out our award nominees, sneak a peek at upcoming titles, and discover the best whodunits each and every month.

Get to know the magnificent mystery authors of HarperCollins and sign up today!